A Bump on a Log

Slocum settled down behind a log and waited. His bleeding back twitched so powerfully he jerked involuntarily. His finger slipped on the trigger and a round whined off into the night. The three gunmen whipped out their six-guns and opened fire, filling the air with lead. One or two bullets thudded into the fallen tree trunk but most sailed past into the woods behind. The road agents had exhausted their six-shooters and then disappeared into the darkness.

Slocum sat up painfully, then used his rifle as a crutch to get to his feet. He stumbled along like an old man to where his Appaloosa still tugged fearfully on the reins.

"Back to Woodchip," he told the horse. Slocum had hardly started back to town when he heard horses behind him in the dark. They might belong to innocent riders, but Slocum wasn't going to bet that way. He got the Appaloosa into a gallop, but the men coming after him began shooting.

He had wondered how he was going to track down the men who had attempted to shoot him out of the saddle. Now he had to worry about staying alive because *they* had found *him* . . .

JAKE LOGAN

SLOCUM
AT WHISKEY LAKE

JOVE BOOKS, NEW YORK

SLOCUM AT WHISKEY LAKE

A Jove Book / published by arrangement with
the author

PRINTING HISTORY
Jove edition / July 2004

Copyright © 2004 by Penguin Group (USA) Inc.

For information, address: The Berkley Publishing Group,
a division of Penguin Group (USA) Inc.,
375 Hudson Street, New York, New York 10014.

ISBN: 0-515-13773-1

A JOVE BOOK®
Jove Books are published by The Berkley Publishing Group,
a division of Penguin Group (USA) Inc.,
375 Hudson Street, New York, New York 10014.
JOVE and the "J" design
are trademarks belonging to Penguin Group (USA) Inc.

PRINTED IN THE UNITED STATES OF AMERICA

10 9 8 7 6 5 4 3 2 1

1

The cool touch of autumn in the Idaho mountains made John Slocum turn up his collar to keep the wind from tickling up and down his spine and giving him a false sense of danger. Slocum had never felt safer or more at peace than now. He pulled down the brim of his Stetson against the bright sun as he wondered why he would ever want to leave such lovely country. But he had to when he was finished with this job. He had accepted a tedious chore down in Wichita and would complete it soon amid the achingly beautiful, wild Bitterroot Mountains before traveling the entire way back to Kansas. The sooner he found Randall Claymore, the sooner he could collect the rest of the considerable sum offered him for a few weeks of his time.

Slocum touched his shirt pocket where almost five hundred dollars in greenbacks rode. He had been promised twice that if he tracked down Claymore, got him to sign legal papers in a dozen or so places then returned the documents to a Wichita lawyer before the middle of November. Slocum wanted the task out of the way long before then because, as cold as it got in the Bitterroot Mountains, the blizzards whipping down out of Canada across the pool table–flat Great Plains would make returning to Wichita even harder. He had been stranded on the rolling, grassy plains that had once been called the Great American Desert one time too many in the dead of winter and had barely escaped with his life.

He had started hunting for Claymore a month ago and had had considerable luck tracking the man from Denver. Slocum felt it in his bones that he was getting close now. Randall Claymore was a gambler and a wastrel and often fancied himself a prospector for gold and other precious metals. All he seemed to find was a passel of trouble, jealous husbands and too many men accusing him of cheating at cards. More than once, the town of Woodchip, Idaho, had been mentioned as a place where Claymore might be headed.

Slocum reined in and let his trusty Appaloosa rest while he drank in the beauty of the area and relished the peacefulness. Too much of his life had been filled with ugliness and sudden death for him not to take a moment to appreciate the land around him. The wind whipped down a valley and brushed across his leathery face like a lover's caress. Seldom had he smelled anything so sweet as the dried leaves and pine scent caught on the wind. It was warm but turning cold. In too short a time that scented air would be a frigid knife stabbing at his lungs unless a warming Chinook happened to blow.

His keen green eyes scanned the double-rutted dirt track stretching ahead of him. His lip curled slightly as he wondered if people in these parts actually considered this a road when it was hardly more than a wide game trail. This valley wound around like a drunk snake and finally coiled up at Woodchip, some ten miles north, with Coeur d'Alene fifteen farther along a much straighter road, if Slocum's informants were right. The forests showed where loggers had worked furiously and then moved on to fresher stands of trees, but that hardly disturbed the overall beauty. Slocum liked this country. If it had been in his nature, he wouldn't have minded staking out a ranch and settling down here.

"I can collect my money and come back in the spring," he said to his horse, patting the stallion on the neck. The Appaloosa whinnied as if approving of the plan. Its breed had come from an area to the west of where Slocum now rode, and this must seem like a homecoming to the animal.

"All I have to do is find Randall Claymore," he finished as a gust of wind threatened to swallow his words. The man was slipperier than an eel and probably fought like a rat when cornered, but Slocum didn't want anything from him but to get the papers signed. The lawyer and others in the Claymore family had all assured him Randall would not hesitate to put his John Hancock down on each and every page because it got him out of some sticky legal mess he had made for himself even as it freed the rest of the family to pursue other business.

Slocum did not consider himself a messenger or a courier or even a process server, but the money had been too good to pass up. And the trail had led him to this peaceful valley nestled in the midst of forests and mountains.

His Appaloosa tried to rear, but he held it down, wondering what had spooked the usually calm horse. Slocum cocked his head to one side and listened hard, figuring he would hear the sound of loggers sawing away or even a miner or two chewing into the side of a mountain as they hunted for the elusive yellow flash of gold. If luck really rode with him, one of those miners would be Randall Claymore.

But Slocum heard nothing of the sort. A faint, weak moan of anguish reached him. He gentled his horse to keep it quiet, then slowly turned his head until he homed in on the sound when it was repeated. A quiet lapping sound mixed with the moaning. Over the hills to his right must be a lake—and someone in big trouble to make such piteous sounds.

Slocum put his heels to the powerful horse's flanks and trotted up the hill where he got a better look at the valley. He shook his head in wonder. On the road, he saw nothing but trees and rocks and had missed how a narrow branch in the valley floor twisted away to the east and held a long, thin finger lake in a gentle bowl. The lake wasn't wide but stretched for what Slocum reckoned was the better part of two miles before vanishing from sight as it wound around yet another jut of mountain. In the middle of the wind-whipped lake, he counted no fewer than three small, lushly overgrown islands.

And on the shore Slocum saw a man stretched out as if trying to reach the water and failing with his dying breath.

"Giddyup," Slocum urged. The horse responded instantly. Slocum galloped downhill to the edge of the lake, dismounting on the run. He dropped to his knees beside the man facedown on the sandy ground, arms reaching futilely toward the lake.

Another loud groan escaped the man's lips.

"Have you been shot?" Slocum asked as he rolled the man over to examine him. While dirty from lying in the mud just beyond the sandy shore, the man seemed unharmed. "What's wrong?"

"Hello, my good man," came the surprisingly cheerful reply. Eyelids flickered open and watery blue eyes stared up at Slocum. "I say, you are a wrangler cowboy, aren't you?"

"I heard you moaning. Did your horse throw you?" Slocum had seen men hit their heads when they landed and be unable to even stand. But such a calamity always left behind a bloody lump on the head. This man was dressed well in what looked like an expensive jacket and fancy pants that clung to his legs as if sewn especially for him. A brocade vest showed a golden chain dangling down. Slocum could see the stem of an expensive watch tucked away in a small, secure pocket. The man had not been thrown nor had he been robbed.

"I say, old man, could you fetch me some water? My horse ran off when I stepped down to relieve myself."

The man sat up and seemed capable enough of getting the water himself. More out of curiosity than concern now, Slocum grabbed his canteen from his saddle and tossed it to the man. The well-dressed man made a face, shrugged then pulled the cork free and sipped daintily at the water. He smacked his lips as if he had been drinking fine whiskey, recorked the canteen and handed it back to Slocum.

"That hit the spot. Thank you."

"Why didn't you get some water from the lake?" Slocum had seen mirages in the desert that confused a man's sense of distance, but he took two steps and got his boots wet in the gently lapping waves kicked up by the wind. It was impossible to believe the lake wasn't real. He knelt and scooped a handful of the water to his lips. "This tastes fine. No trace of alkali in it."

"Oh, I suppose it is quite good water." The man smiled winningly. "It probably tastes rather good, actually, but it hardly lives up to its name."

"What's that?" asked Slocum, still wondering what was going on.

"Whiskey Lake, old chap. They call this Whiskey Lake."

"Have miners been dumping their tailings into the lake and poisoned it?" Slocum asked, still wondering why the man hadn't crawled the last six feet to get his own drink. He wasn't injured and appeared to be possessed of his senses, although Slocum found the British accent a bit hard to follow.

"Not that I know of, although many of those fellows burrow away like moles in the mountains around here. If there's not some bloke cutting down a tree, then there's another one digging away furiously. The whole region is quite crowded, though it hardly looks it."

"Why the hell didn't you get your own drink?" Slocum burst out.

"I lost my cup, of course," the man said with a straight face.

Slocum stared at him incredulously, wondering if he was the butt of some joke, but the man sounded sincere.

"I am James Barrington-Finch, but everyone in these parts calls me Finch." He got to his feet and thrust out his hand. Slocum shook it mechanically, still trying to decide if the man meant it.

"You weren't dying of thirst, were you?" Slocum asked as Finch pumped his hand in a strong grip.

"Why, yes, I was. But I explained why I didn't partake of the water from Whiskey Lake. I do so hope my horse returns to its stable where I can regain my belongings. The tack isn't worth much, but it is all I have."

"Where might your horse go?" Slocum asked, still staring at Finch. The man was a few inches shorter than Slocum's six-foot height, had sandy hair and eyes such a pale blue that they almost vanished. The water in Whiskey Lake was bluer. Finch had a long, thin nose and sported sunburned cheeks, betraying how little he had been outdoors and that when he had been, the bright Idaho sun had clearly taken its toll on pale flesh. The man's handshake was firm, but Slocum had the feeling that there wasn't much in the way of muscle under Finch's fancy duds.

"I am staying in Woodchip, a delightfully quaint little hamlet some miles from here." Finch waved his hand around, vaguely pointing in the right direction.

"I'm heading in that way. You can ride behind me, unless you want to stay to hunt for your horse."

"Goodness, no, I am certain that magnificently sway-backed beast of burden has already returned to its stable. You see, I am merely renting the horse from the livery-man."

Slocum mounted, then reached down and gave Finch a helping hand up. The man settled behind Slocum comfortably. At least there didn't seem to be any danger of him falling off. Slocum got the Appaloosa into a walk and retraced his path up the hill and back down to the road.

"How remarkable," Finch said. "I was so close to the road and never knew it. I was turned about, you see, and thought I was at the *other* end of the lake. It is quite nice that you showed up to save me the way you did, old chap."

Slocum rode along in silence, wondering if Finch had a keeper and if so, why that keeper ever let him slip free of his leash. The man lacked even rudimentary frontier skills, other than horsemanship.

"There's the outskirts of Woodchip," Finch called as he eagerly pointed to a battered sign that had once been painted in bright canary-yellow letters. Wind and rain had faded the lettering and termites had feasted for at least one season on the tasty wood beneath. Still, Slocum hardly needed Finch to tell him they had arrived at a boom-town.

"Not much in the way of mining around here, is there?" asked Slocum. He saw only one saloon at the edge of town as he rode down the muddy main street. If there had been even a hint of a big strike, the town would have boasted a dozen or more gin mills, all packed to overflowing with thirsty miners.

"That's true," Finch agreed. "Now, those chaps who fell the tall trees . . ."

"The lumberjacks," supplied Slocum when it became obvious Finch was struggling to find the right word.

"Well, I suppose you can call them that. I call them filthy sons of bitches. They divide their time between Woodchip and another spot farther north."

"How come you don't cotton much to them?"

"Cotton? Ah, yes, why don't I like them? They are a scurrilous lot and are prone to make fun of me."

"Fancy that," Slocum said dryly.

"I require a tot of fine brandy to get the taste of the water from my lips. Could we stop so I could indulge myself? No offense, Mr. Slocum, but the water in your canteen is most foul."

"No offense taken," Slocum said, stopping in front of the Fancy Lady Saloon and letting Finch dismount. He quickly followed. "Fact is, I don't like the taste myself, not when I can have some whiskey."

"Spoken like a true gentleman. Come, sir, enter this fine establishment and I shall stand you to that aqua vitae. The best Miss Maude has to offer!"

With a grand gesture, Finch charged up the sagging board steps and made a grand entrance, Slocum following a few steps behind to watch the show. He was amused at the Brit, but he had a job to finish. The best place in Woodchip to hunt for Randall Claymore was right here in the Fancy Lady.

"Two goblets of your finest beverages, my good man!" Finch went to the bar and thumped his fist until the mahogany pane rang.

"You ain't paid your tab from last month yet, Finch," the barkeep growled. "No more credit till you fork over the dough."

"Credit! Why, this is an outrage! You know I am good for the measly amount of my bill. Come the first of the month, there will be that paltry sum and more to buy liquor!"

"That's all right," Slocum said, seeing the bartender

wasn't going to budge. "I'll buy this round. You can get one later."

"Lemme see the color of your gold, mister," the barkeep said. He frowned when Slocum peeled off a few greenbacks and reluctantly made them vanish under the bar before bringing out a bottle. Like most places, paying in scrip was frowned on but Slocum wasn't going to waste what hard coin he had on drinking.

Faster than a striking rattler, Finch grabbed the bartender's wrist and stopped him from pouring.

"Not that tarantula juice, Sidney my man. The good stuff. The whiskey that at least pretends it has been near the glorious state of Kentucky."

"All I got's Billy Taylor's Finest," the barkeep said.

"Then that is what I shall serve my good friend," Finch said, as if he were the one buying.

Slocum watched in amusement as the bartender fetched a bottle with an amber liquid that might actually have been Kentucky whiskey. From the bite and the smooth feel as it swirled down his gullet, if it wasn't genuine it was the best fake Slocum had ever swilled.

"Good," Slocum said, setting the shot glass on the bar and wiping his lips. "Thanks."

"Thank you for your charity, sir, in rescuing me and in quenching my blast furnace of a thirst." Finch turned around and rested his elbows on the bar as he looked out across the wide but shallow barroom. "Ah, another friend of mine!"

With that Finch was off. It took Slocum a couple seconds to realize Finch had absconded with the entire bottle of whiskey. Before he could say anything, the barkeep was in front of him.

"You got to pay for the whole damn bottle. No way you're gonna pry that from his hand until he's fallin'-down drunk."

"I take it I'm not the first, uh, friend who's had this

happen," Slocum said, smiling. The Britisher amused him, and he couldn't figure out why. Slocum wasn't the sort to let deadbeats sponge off him, but Finch had a pleasant air about him that made it almost tolerable. He paid for the bottle, intending to go rescue a drink or two for himself.

His attention was drawn away from the matter by a burly man dressed in tattered, patched canvas pants and a black-and-red-checked flannel shirt that branded him as a logger. The lumberjack towered over a petite brunette who stood with her back to Slocum. As the logger leaned over the woman, Slocum couldn't help noticing how she held her ground without so much as flinching.

"You and me, Maude, what say we go on upstairs and have a tumble or two?"

"No," the woman said firmly, poking the man in the center of his broad chest with her index finger. "You're not my type."

"What ya gonna do if I grab you by that fine, long hair of yours and drag you upstairs?"

"I'd strap on a gun and blow your balls off," she said in a level tone. From the way she stood and spoke, Slocum doubted this was any idle threat on her part.

"A gun'd look real good on that hip of yours," the lumberjack said, reaching out to put his dirty hand on her.

Maude stepped closer, but her hands didn't go for the logger's hip. She grabbed his crotch. From where he stood Slocum saw the muscles on the woman's shoulders knot with strain. The logger turned pale and tried to step back. Maude followed him, keeping her grip.

"Apologize," she said in the same level tone.

"Y-yes, Maude," he gasped out. "I-I'm sure sorry."

"Get out of here," she said, shoving him hard enough to knock him down. "Don't come back till you've sobered up and know how to treat a lady!" Maude turned and Slocum saw her face for the first time. He caught his breath. He had not expected such a lovely woman to have the presence to back down a drunk lumberjack the way she had.

"What are you staring at?" she said, chocolate eyes fixing on Slocum's green ones.

"I'd say 'a beautiful woman', but seeing what you just did, I don't think I'm up to taking such punishment."

Maude glanced at the logger getting to his feet and stumbling from the Fancy Lady. Then she turned back to Slocum and said, "Don't worry. You're my type."

"Lucky me," Slocum said.

"No," Maude said drawing out the word into a long syllable. "Lucky me. Buy me a drink and tell me exactly how beautiful you think I am."

Slocum laughed. There was genuine humor in the woman's tone as she joshed him.

"Another bottle," Slocum ordered.

"Wait, Sid," she said, stopping the barkeep from reaching for the bottle on the back bar. "What's he mean, 'another bottle?' "

"He a'ready bought Finch one."

"Do tell? A gentleman *and* an easy mark. Then this drink's on me." Maude faced down the disapproving barkeep.

"Thanks," Slocum said, knocking back the drink. If anything, this whiskey was even smoother than what he had bought for the Britisher.

"How'd you happen on Finch?" Maude asked. She moved closer. The hip she had promised to strap a six-shooter on now rubbed seductively against Slocum's leg. Maude was short, hardly an inch over five feet, but she squeezed a lot of woman into that small package.

Slocum told how he had found the man dying of thirst on the bank of the lake. This produced a gale of laughter.

"He wouldn't even stick his damn fool head in because he'd lost his silver goblet? That's rich, that's really rich."

Maude laughed until tears came to her eyes. "Stories like this are why I let the limey run his bill up."

"What's he do to make a living?" Slocum asked. "The whole way into Woodchip he never mentioned a job."

"He's a remittance man."

"What's that?" Slocum looked into Maude's fathomless brown eyes and found he didn't care about James Barrington-Finch at all. He just wanted to keep Maude talking so he could enjoy her company a few more minutes.

"He never talks much about his family back in England, but he's not the first son and isn't going to inherit the family fortune or title. He'll never be the second Lord Barrington-Finch or one more than whatever his father's called now. That's reserved for Finch's older brother. So they shipped him out rather than keeping him around the estate to cause trouble and embarrass them."

"They sent him to America?"

"Why not? Let him make his fortune on his own out here, but with some help. The first of every month Finch gets a sizable transfer drawn on a St. Louis bank. As long as the money comes, he stays out of the family business back in England, whatever that might be. Finch's never said. In a way, they all get what they want."

"So he gets this remittance and that's what he lives off? No job?"

"Not that I've ever seen. He talks about all kinds of wild things, but he never carries through with any of them."

"What kind of wild things?" asked Slocum.

"Going into farming or ranching. Running a thousand head of cattle. Getting into politics and being governor of the territory, things like that. Crazy things. Finch is a nice guy, but I can't see him sticking with anything longer than a day or two." Maude eyed Slocum from head to toe and back, her eyes lingering on the worn ebony butt of his Colt Navy. "You a gunslinger?"

"No," Slocum said flatly.

"I see," Maude said, hearing the unspoken order in his answer to not pursue the matter.

Slocum heard a loud crash and spun, his hand reaching for the six gun. He stopped when he saw that Finch had fallen out of his chair and lay on the floor on his side.

"He's not hurt," Maude said. "He'll pick himself up and walk on out of here in a minute or two. Wait and see."

Slocum and Maude watched in silence as Finch stirred, got his feet under him then tried to smooth wrinkles from his fancy coat. With all the dignity of a lord, he walked to the door, missed and slammed into the wall, spun and faced the room.

"A dutiful g-good night to one and all," he stuttered.

"Don't let the door hit you in the ass," Sid the barkeep called.

"Good night, Finch," Maude called. "You sure you can get home all right?"

"Of c-course, my dear Miss Maude. Th-thank you for c-caring. I know my way." With dignity only a drunk can muster, Finch made it through the door and out into the cold Idaho night.

"He ought to be halfway toward sober by the time he gets to the stables," Maude said.

"That's where he sleeps?"

"There's not much in the way of hotels in Woodchip, if you hadn't noticed."

Slocum started to ask where he might sleep—or at least spend the night—when he heard a loud cry from outside.

"That's Finch!" Slocum lit out running and got to the saloon doors in time to see a man standing over Finch. As the drunken Britisher tried to wiggle away, the man cocked back his fist and then punched down into Finch's belly. Finch gasped and curled up.

"Gimme that fancy watch," the man growled. He jerked at Finch's coat and ripped it as he searched for the watch hidden away in a vest pocket.

"Touch it and you'll regret it," Slocum said. His six-shooter came easily to his hand. The sound of the gun cocking echoed along the suddenly still street.

The would-be thief stepped away from his victim, stared at Slocum for an instant, then bolted like a frightened rabbit.

"You all right, Finch?" Slocum called. He kept the fleeing thief in his sights until the man ducked around the corner of the town bakery a half dozen buildings down the street and vanished.

"I am fine, Mr. Slocum. T-that's t-twice in one day you have saved me. I should have known better than to allow myself to be beset like that, especially by a brigand like Claymore."

"What did you say?"

"I said, I should have—"

"No, no," Slocum said, shaking Finch to sober him up a mite. "You called him by name. Do you know him?"

"Claymore? Of course I know him. A worthless scoundrel, if ever I've seen one."

"Randall Claymore?"

"I believe that is his moniker."

Slocum released Finch, who stumbled and sat heavily in the street. Slocum took a few steps in the direction Claymore had fled, then stopped.

"Do you know where he hangs out?" Slocum asked.

His only answer was a weak retching as Finch lost all the fine booze he had poured down his gullet earlier— that Slocum had paid for.

"Come on," Slocum said, getting a wobbly Finch to his feet. "I'll get you settled down at the stables."

"You are a prince among m-men, sir," Finch got out before puking again.

Slocum made certain he held Finch so the man's head was always turned away. This was disagreeable duty but in spite of it, Slocum felt a glow of success. He had found Randall Claymore.

All he had to do was get on his trail and he could get the papers signed before sunup.

2

"Are you sure you're all right?" Slocum asked Barrington-Finch as they entered the livery stable. The Britisher rubbed his head, then his bruised arm and finally nodded.

"Nothing seems to have shaken loose." Finch smiled wryly and added, "Except for the contents of my tummy."

"Are you sure the man who attacked you was Randall Claymore?"

"Why, as certain as the Cross of St. Andrew is on the Union Jack," Finch replied. Slocum didn't know how sure that was and hesitated. Finch went on in a conversational tone, as if nothing had happened. "I don't think you should fetch that annoying sheriff and tell him of this contretemps. It is nothing, a mere trifle. There was naught Claymore could filch from me, save for my watch, and it is right where it ought to be." Finch took it out, popped open the gold cover and peered drunkenly at the face.

"I say, it is past midnight. I must get my beauty sleep."

Finch clicked shut the case and fell back into a stall onto sweet-smelling hay intended to feed the animals. He was asleep before Slocum could say another word.

"So I had Claymore in the palm of my hand and let him go," Slocum muttered. Still, the encounter had proven

16

lucky for him. He now knew Randall Claymore was in the vicinity and what he looked like. All he had to do was track him down. Slocum hurried back to the Fancy Lady Saloon on the outskirts of town and grabbed the reins of his horse. Mounting before the Appaloosa could turn away from the hitching post, Slocum put his heels to the horse's flanks and got it trotting in the direction taken by the fleeing Claymore.

Slocum rounded the building where the would-be sneak-thief had disappeared and immediately found how difficult it would be tracking down Claymore. The ground was dusty and didn't hold tracks worth a damn. He jumped down and studied the ground, then looked up. If Claymore had kept running in this direction he would have gone into a stand of juniper some distance from town. Lacking any other hint to the man's whereabouts, Slocum walked forward slowly, his grateful horse trailing him.

When he reached the stand of trees, Lady Luck again smiled on him. He had no trouble finding where a horse had been tethered for some time, by the look of the still-warm piles of manure. The tracks leading away were partially hidden by leaves, fallen pine needles and other debris from the forest but Slocum had a good idea where Claymore headed.

He remained on foot to keep from banging his head on the low juniper limbs and finally came to an open area. In the dark it was hard to tell but he thought it might be a mountain meadow. And the road into Woodchip curled around and went past the far side of the meadow. Slocum mounted and trotted across the grassy stretch, trusting his horse not to find a gopher hole and break a leg in the dark.

When he reached the road, skill replaced luck and let him find the indistinct outline of a horse's recent hoofprint. Slocum listened hard but could not hear the sound

of a galloping horse in the distance. That didn't mean
Claymore wasn't hurrying away at this very moment.
With the winding canyons and forested slopes to soak up
the sounds, he might have to get Claymore in his sights
before he could hear anything useful.

Slocum trotted his horse along the double ruts in the
road, sure he was closing the gap between him and Claymore. He had visions of persuading Claymore to sign the
papers and being back in Woodchip at the Fancy Lady
Saloon before Maude closed up for the night.

That would be the perfect way to wind up the day and
his search for Randall Claymore.

As he rode, Slocum's mind drifted and he became less
attentive to his surroundings. The moon poked half a face
up over the mountains to the east and gave a liquid appearance to the land that he found engrossing. Too engrossing.

It took Slocum a second to realize the sound he heard
was that of a hammer cocking on a six-shooter. It took
him another second to react, and that slowness almost cost
him his life.

Slocum threw himself forward so he hugged the
horse's neck. He felt a hot flash of lightning surge the
length of his back as the bullet tore past. The sudden pain
almost unseated him. He clung to the saddle horn grimly
as the pain receded a little, but he could do nothing to
stop the frightened horse from galloping ahead.

He shook off the shock of being shot and regained
control so he could get the horse away from the road and
to cover, away from the sights of whoever had tried to
ambush him.

Slocum eased the horse in a jump over a fallen log and
into a stand of piñons, where he dismounted. He grunted
in pain as he moved, the blood running steadily from the
long, shallow crease the gunman had put into his back.
For the moment there was nothing he could do about the

wound other than let his shirt sop up the blood.

Pulling his Winchester from the saddle sheath and levering in a round made him feel better. If anyone foolishly showed himself now, he'd be a goner. During the war Slocum had been a sniper for the South, and a good one. He had learned patience early on so he could sit all day in the crotch of a tree limb waiting for the flash of a brass button or gold braid on a Union officer's uniform. A single shot from his rifle had determined the course of battle more than once for his unit.

Without a leader, a military element tended to mill about aimlessly.

Right now, Slocum intended to do more than let his attacker mill about. He wanted the son of a bitch in his sights so he could put him six feet under.

Slocum settled down behind the termite-infested log and waited, the moon rising higher in the sky. The angle of the moon worked against him, illuminating him rather than the sniper, but Slocum never moved a muscle even when his back began to spasm in pain. The bleeding had stopped when the blood clotted over, but the wound itself made for increasing discomfort. But he held his position, unmoving, as alert as he could possibly be.

Slocum's finger tightened on the trigger when he saw movement out on the road. Then he relaxed when it occurred to him that he dared not shoot Claymore. He needed the man's signature if he wanted to collect another thousand dollars back in Wichita. That meant he had to get the signature before he evened the score, because he wasn't going to let a cowardly thief like Claymore gun him down and get away with it.

Slocum's eyes narrowed when he saw a second rider join the first. Then a third joined his partners. Seeing the gang together but being unable to identify them presented a dilemma for Slocum. He might have been ambushed by a gang of road agents rather than Randall Claymore. Or

Claymore might be part of the gang. Slocum couldn't tell because the moon shone full against his face and cloaked the three riders in deep ebony shadows.

Not sure what to do, fate intruded again on Slocum to decide the issue. His back twitched so powerfully he jerked involuntarily. His finger slipped on the trigger and a round whined off into the night. The bullet went nowhere near the three gunmen, but it alerted them. They whipped out their six-guns and opened fire, filling the air with enough lead to drive Slocum back behind the log for shelter.

One or two bullets thudded into the fallen tree trunk but most sailed past into the woods behind. He heard his Appaloosa whinny in fear as one slug came too close, but he didn't think the animal had been hit. He chanced a quick look up, intending to return fire.

The moonlit road stretched out into the darkness, as empty as could be. The road agents had exhausted their six-shooters and then disappeared into the darkness.

Slocum sat up painfully, then used his rifle as a crutch to get to his feet. He stumbled along like an old man to where his Appaloosa still tugged fearfully on the reins.

"Calm down," Slocum said in a soothing voice, knowing the horse was frightened and unwilling—and unable—to do much about it. He shoved his rifle into its sheath, grabbed the saddle horn and cantle and pulled himself up. For a moment, he sat upright. Then dizziness hit him. Slocum almost fell from the saddle, but he fought to keep from passing out as waves of pain stabbed through his body.

"Back to Woodchip," he told the horse. He hardly knew when the Appaloosa began walking, but Slocum did his best to keep an eye out for the men who had tried to ventilate him. Claymore might be with them or the sneak-thief might still be running, scared for his life.

Slocum had hardly started back to town when he heard

horses behind him in the dark. They might belong to innocent riders, but Slocum wasn't going to bet that way. He got the Appaloosa into a gallop, but the men coming after him began shooting. He had wondered how he was going to track down the men who had attempted to shoot him out of the saddle. Now he had to worry about staying alive because they had found him again.

"Get him. He's gettin' away!" shouted one rider.

"You done winged the varmint. Lookit the way he's draped over in the saddle. We got him!"

"Shaddap," growled the third man. Slocum pegged him as the leader, not that it did any good. He couldn't tell who was who as he bent low to present as small a target as possible. The lead continued to fly around him as he rode. Slocum began cursing himself for being such a fool. There was no reason he should have expected the trio to ride away after taking a few shots at him behind the log. They had ridden off and waited for him to show himself— and he had done so like some greenhorn.

It became apparent he wasn't going to outrun the three gunmen.

"Get ready, old boy," Slocum whispered to the Appaloosa. The whites showed around the horse's eyes, giving mute testimony to how frightened the stallion was. Slocum knew the horse was going to be a lot more spooked in a minute.

Then he slipped from the saddle, hit the ground with bone-jarring force and rolled into a ditch a yard away from the road. Slocum lay still on his belly as his horse raced off into the night.

"We got him! I tole you so. We done nailed his ass good!"

"Shaddap," came the order from the leader. "Let's make sure he's dead. We don't want more of them pokin' their noses where they don't belong."

The three walked over and stopped a dozen paces from where Slocum lay unmoving.

"Put a bullet in him, just to be sure," the leader ordered.

"He's dead, boss. See? He's not movin' a muscle. And look at the back of his danged shirt! I musta drilled him plumb through his carcass for there to be that much blood."

"Shoot him, or I'll shoot you."

"Aw, boss."

Slocum moved like an uncoiling steel spring. He rolled onto his back, ignoring the vicious pain that caused his eyes to blur for a moment, then started shooting at the trio. His first two shots went high. When he found the range he was rewarded with a yelp of pain as he winged first one, then another of the three men.

The one he reckoned to be the boss slapped leather and got his six-gun out and firing, but Slocum had reserved a couple rounds for him. The gunman was shooting in panic, his bullets going wild. Slocum was more in control. Both of his shots found targets. The man let out a tiny gasp and sagged.

"Get out of here!" shouted one of the others. From the way the other two moved, Slocum knew he hadn't killed them. But he had given as good as he had got. They were in a world of hurt, just as he was.

He reached into his pocket, pulled out a loaded cylinder and replaced the one in his Colt Navy. By the time he lifted the freshly loaded gun and got off another shot, the three men were riding hell-bent for leather out of range. He emptied the cylinder after them to keep them from coming back.

Slocum sank to the ground, fought back the red waves of pain that rose within him and carefully replaced the cylinder again with the last of his loaded spares. He didn't want to be at the highwaymen's mercy, should they be foolish enough to return.

Whistling the best he could, Slocum waited for the Appaloosa. The horse didn't come right away, but he waited. There wasn't anything else he could do. Walking back to Woodchip was out of the question in his condition.

Finally, he heard the familiar snort and whinny, got to his feet and caught at the horse as it skittishly approached him. Again forcing himself to forget the pain, Slocum mounted and started once more for town. As he rode the pain diminished. He wasn't sure if the worst was in the past or just beginning.

He had been wounded enough times to know the signs that he was in danger. While a tad light-headed, he wasn't wobbling in the saddle as he rode. There wasn't any tingling in his arms or legs, and his head didn't ring like a church bell. Best of all for him, he wasn't cold from loss of blood and shock. His wound was messy but not serious, and the tiredness he felt was more from the letdown after a gunfight than from losing much blood.

The night wasn't as beguiling as it had been, and Slocum ruefully admitted he had been too optimistic about finding Claymore. That wouldn't happen again. He didn't know if the man was one of the gang that had shot him up, but he would proceed after Claymore as if it were true. Claymore had to stay alive long enough to sign the papers, but Slocum had said nothing about what condition he would leave the man in.

If Claymore had any part in the ambush, he and his cronies would pay for it. Slocum would see to it.

As he rode down the solitary main street of Woodchip, he heard loud shouts and crashes from the Fancy Lady Saloon at the far end of town. He needed to find the marshal or the sheriff to report being ambushed, but if there was that much ruckus coming from the saloon, any law-man in town was likely to be there.

Besides, Slocum needed a stiff shot of whiskey to ease his pain. He could kill two birds with one stone by going to the saloon.

As he rode up, a table came sailing through a plate-glass window at the front of the saloon. Glass splinters and the table rattled on the boardwalk and then skidded into the street. A chair went through the other window facing the street. From inside the saloon came a din that made the breaking glass sound like a whisper in church.

"Stop it," he heard Sid shout. A meaty thud silenced the barkeep.

"You didn't have any call to do that, you mangy Cay-use!" This was Maude's voice. When she yelped in pain, Slocum knew he had to act. He patted the six-shooter in its cross-draw holster, made sure he hadn't simply imag-ined reloading it, then slid from the saddle.

His legs wobbled as he walked, but he got to the door. Someone had ripped it off its hinges and to that it hung askew.

"Let her go," Slocum called, hand resting on the ebony butt of his six-gun.

For a moment, dead silence fell inside the Fancy Lady. Slocum knew he presented quite a horrific sight, all caked in blood as he was. But he knew it was the iron edge in his voice that froze the man trying to pin Maude against the bar.

"Slocum!" Maude cried. "What's happened to you?"

"Never mind that. Come on over here."

"No," the man holding her said. "We're not done here yet."

"You're plenty done," Slocum said, half drawing his Colt.

"Pull it and you're a dead man." Maude's assailant

turned and faced Slocum squarely. A star gleaned in the light on his chest.

Slocum froze, caught on the edge of a dilemma. Did he throw down on a lawman or did he surrender and let the sheriff continue breaking up the saloon and manhandling Maude?

3

Slocum came to a quick decision. He stepped forward and bumped hard into the lawman, knocking the sheriff back a pace. The sheriff's face turned into a thundercloud of anger as he drew back his lips in a feral snarl.

"What call do you have interferin' with legal business?" The sheriff's hand rested on his six-shooter now.

Slocum turned slightly to put himself more completely between the lawman and Maude. He heard the woman gasp when she saw his bloody shirt, but he ignored her reaction.

"I was ambushed out on the road, Sheriff," Slocum said. "I got shot and—"

"And hell, mister. Outta my way. I got business to tend to here, legal business." The sheriff grabbed Slocum as he had Maude but this time the reaction was different. Slocum's hand shot out as fast as a striking snake and took the man's wrist in a powerful grip. Slocum twisted to the side and slammed the sheriff into the bar. Hard.

The ruckus in the rest of the Fancy Lady Saloon died to a whisper and then complete silence reigned. Slocum heard a lovesick coyote howling outside and the rustle of autumn winds trying hard to turn into a wintery gale. But inside there was only the sound of the lawman's harsh breathing and the thudding of Slocum's pulse in his own ears.

"I'm gonna run you in for strikin' a peace officer," the sheriff shouted. He rubbed his wrist. "Joshua, Pete, throw this son of a bitch into jail!"

"I slipped, Sheriff. I was ambushed on the road and losing so much blood's made me a bit woozy." Slocum turned to lean on the bar. It felt good to take some of the weight off his feet this way, but he wanted the sheriff to see how blood-caked his shirt was, in explanation of him striking a lawman.

"I don't care if the Queen o' England raped you. You can't go shovin' William Clancy Pennant around!"

"Sheriff, he's mighty shot up," said one deputy. "I ain't never seen nobody that bloody what didn't up and die real soon."

"Then he's gonna die in my calaboose!" roared the sheriff.

Slocum glanced at Maude. She was caught between keeping quiet and speaking up for Slocum. The lovely brunette slipped around Slocum and shoved her finger hard into Sheriff Pennant's chest.

"You look here, you miserable cur," Maude raged. "You can go bust up my saloon. I can't stop you, and you're just doing what most of the citizens of this town want. But this gent's hurt bad. You got eyes. Look at him!"

"All I see is a stranger willing to go to jail," Pennant said, but Slocum heard how the sheriff's voice changed subtly. He was still mad as a wet hen, but Maude was talking sense to him.

"Go on, tear up my place in the name of your religion, but you either leave him alone or get him a doctor. That's the only Christian thing to do for a fellow this badly hurt."

"Josh, why're you stoppin'?" Pennant growled. "Keep

bustin' up them kegs. I don't want a drop of that witch's brew left. It's the devil's own work bein' served in this hellhole. Bust up all the kegs! You, too, Pete Rawlins. Nothin's to be left!"

Slocum started to ask what was going on but a shake of Maude's head quieted him. She knew the local politics better than he did. If she had crossed the lawman, all that would happen would be losing her liquor supply. That was more easily replaced than getting free if she—and Slocum—got thrown into jail.

"That's 'bout it, Sheriff," called Pete, holding up an ax dripping whiskey.

"Joshua?" Sheriff Pennant glared in the other deputy's direction.

"All done, sir," Josh answered. "There's nary a drop of demon rum left to tempt the lost souls of Woodchip."

Pennant jerked his head toward the door and stalked out. His two deputies followed. Slocum had to smile when he saw Josh open his coat to show the other deputy a small bottle of whiskey he had filched. The sheriff might be on a crusade to destroy Maude's rotgut but his deputies would enjoy a drink or two later.

"What happened to you? You look like a herd of buffalo ran over you!" exclaimed Maude. She took Slocum by the arm and guided him to the only chair nearby that hadn't been smashed by the deputies in their haste to get to the whiskey barrels.

"I tried to tell the sheriff. Got ambushed." Slocum sat in the chair and felt all his strength flow out of him.

"Sid, get some of that whiskey over here."

"Sorry, Maude. The sheriff done a real good job this time. He even found the stash hidden under the bar."

"Get Doc Goldberg, then. Mr. Slocum's in a sorry way."

"Wait, no need," Slocum said. "I'm feeling better. I rode back, didn't I?"

"How's this feel?" Maude asked. She grabbed a double handful of his shirt, hesitated long enough for Slocum to feel her fingernails cut into his flesh, then she yanked. Hard. Slocum bit back a scream of pain. The saloon turned a bit dark for a few seconds, then he regained his senses.

"I've got to admit that I've felt better," he got out.

"I took a fair amount of skin with the shirt," Maude said, showing no sympathy. "You know what, Slocum? For all the blood, there's not a hell of a lot of wound. You bled like a stuck pig but probably won't even have a scar to show for it."

"Good," Slocum said. "I've got plenty already."

"I see that." She bent close and whispered in his ear. "You don't move or I will skin you alive." Maude straightened, brushed the brown hair from her eyes and looked around the devastated saloon. "Sid, don't bother with this unholy mess right now. Tomorrow's good enough."

"Why bother, Maude? We don't have any whiskey. And if you get more, the sheriff's only goin' to slop it all over the floorboards again. The Mormons in town must be really puttin' it to him to keep out all the liquor."

"This is the third time Pennant's done this," Maude said in disgust. "He's not going to stop. And I'm not, either!"

Slocum leaned forward on a table, his elbows supporting his weight. Cool wind came through a broken window and drifted across his feverish back. Other than a dull ache left from Maude's precipitous removal of his shirt, he didn't feel too bad.

"You're a danged fool to do it, Maude. That's why I work for you." Sid grinned, showed a bright gold tooth, then put on his hat, dropped a filthy apron on the end of the bar and left. The saloon became quieter and somehow lonelier.

Maude closed the doors the best she could, propping up one with a chair. She dusted off her hands and came back to the table where Slocum still leaned forward to take the pressure off his back.

"You look like hell," she said.

"You look fabulous," Slocum replied. "I can't say it was worth getting shot up to have you rip off my shirt, but it goes a ways toward making it better."

"Would me taking off the rest of your clothes make it better?" Maude looked at him, her brown eyes dancing with merriment.

"Only if you take off yours, too," Slocum said.

"I knew you were my type when I first laid eyes on you, but that's not what I want laid right now," she said, moving closer to Slocum. Maude reached out and gently pressed her hand against his stubbled cheek. Her fingers tightened on the side of his head so she could rock it back, get his lips turned up and kiss them hard.

Slocum had thought he was at the end of his rope but found new strength flooding into him. Everything about the woman gave him new energy. He reached up and put his arms around Maude and drew her down so she sat across his lap. Their kiss deepened until they were both gasping for breath.

As Maude drew back, she exposed her neck to Slocum's eager kisses. He worked his way down from her slender throat to the deep valley between her breasts. He licked and kissed and tried to work his tongue under the stiff edge of her dress.

"You *are* weak if you can't get 'em out where your mouth can do 'em some good," Maude declared. She reached behind her, fumbled a moment and loosened the tight dress. Slocum saw the bodice sag a little and then the woman's ample breasts came tumbling out.

White and succulent, they bobbed only a little as he worked to the pointed tip of the one closest to him. His questing lips caught the warm, rubbery coral nub at the crest and sucked it hard into his mouth. As he began running his tongue over the sensitive tip, Maude let out a low, soft, moan of stark delight.

"You are really getting to me, John. I don't let men get this close, but you know how to do it all, don't you?"

He answered with his mouth—but without speaking. He quickly jumped to the other firmly fleshed breast and duplicated his oral attention. He drew the firm cap of her nipple into his mouth and used his teeth to lightly rake the edges. This caused Maude to shudder just a little.

She clung to him, as if she wanted to shove her entire breast into his mouth. Slocum wouldn't have minded, though it was more than a mouthful. For such a little lady, she was well endowed. He lapped and licked and sucked and then slowly worked his way into the deep canyon between those fleshy mountains.

"No more, John. No more, please," panted Maude.

"You mean it?"

"Not here. I'm cramping your style."

"Not that I noticed," he said. Then Slocum gasped when she reached down to his crotch and grabbed. He remembered the way she had handled the drunk earlier in the evening. Her grip was more gentle now, but it left nothing to Slocum's imagination. He knew what Maude wanted.

The same as he did.

"I got a room upstairs. It's not much but it's got a bed. That's better than banging our brains out here, even if the smell's not half bad." She laughed at this as she stood.

Slocum took a deep whiff of the whisky vapor and found it almost enough to get drunk on. Or was it the sight of Maude naked to the waist that made his head spin so? He reached for her, but she lightly danced away, just beyond his grasp.

Maude pirouetted, and as she turned her skirts came

free. She lithely stepped out of them, clad only in lacy bloomers that hid nothing of her charms. He saw the sleek curve of her ass, the strong, slender legs and even hints of the dark fleecy patch nestled between them. She kept turning and working the bloomers down until he was treated to the sight of her naked rump.

She bent over, facing away from him so he got an even better view.

"Why, John, I do believe you're staring. Didn't anyone ever tell you that wasn't polite?"

"What I want to do isn't polite."

"Then let's go where we won't be disturbed as we get positively unmannerly with each other."

Maude dashed to the stairs leading to a darkened second floor. She paused, turned just enough to give Slocum a view of a delectable breast, a firm thigh and short but well-turned legs. Then she hurried upstairs. He wasted no time going after her.

He reached the top of the stairs and found the light from below penetrated only a few feet down the narrow corridor. Slocum looked for the delightfully naked woman but didn't see her.

"Where'd you go?" he called.

"Find me," came the teasing answer.

Slocum tried one room after another, getting lewd comments about his lack of progress, but he knew he was getting closer. The last room he came to had to be Maude's bedroom. A large four-poster bed dominated the room, but Slocum didn't see the woman anywhere.

"Maude?" He stepped into the room and knew right away he had come to the right place. He felt the sultry brunette step up behind him. She kicked shut the door as she reached around his waist. Her hands moved lower as he stood stock-still for her. Nimble fingers unfastened his gun belt and let it crash to the floor. Then she worked on the buttons on his jeans. One by one the brass buttons popped free until his steely manhood jutted out proudly from his groin.

Then Maude took it in hand and began stroking.

"That feel good?"

"Makes me forget about damned near everything," Slocum admitted.

He felt her firm breasts slipping seductively against his back, carefully missing the spot where the bullet had creased him. Then she sank down lower but never took her hands off his thick stalk, never slowed the stroking, never stopped giving him electric tremors throughout his loins. Maude dropped to her knees behind and began kissing him in this position.

Slocum felt his legs turn weak.

"Go on, lean on the bed, but stand with your legs spread wide," Maude said. Slocum did as he was told, wondering what he was in for. He found out fast.

The woman turned behind him, then came up facing him from between his legs. Her pursed, ruby lips brushed over the tip of his throbbing stalk before she moved up to lie on the bed. Her breasts lightly touched his turgid organ as she made her way up into the circle of his arms. Again they kissed but this time Slocum leaned forward even more and pushed Maude flat on her back onto the soft mattress.

"Umm, so nice," she cooed. Her hands roved over his strong arms and across his shoulders, lightly touching his back to keep from aggravating his wound.

"It'll get nicer in a second," Slocum promised. He reached under her on the bed and cupped her buttocks. With a surge of power, he lifted her and deposited her in the center of the bed so she rocked back and forth.

"Ride 'em, cowboy," Maude cried, lifting her legs on either side of Slocum's body as he scrambled onto the bed. She gasped when he thrust forward, hitting the moist, soft target squarely. "Ride *me*, cowboy," she gasped out.

That was Slocum's intent. He positioned himself better on the softly yielding bed, found his balance and then smoothly stroked forward until he was buried balls-deep in her clinging, moist center.

They both gasped with the power and depth of his penetration. For a moment, Slocum hung suspended. Then he pulled back slowly, enjoying the feel every inch of the way. Maude trembled beneath him like a leaf caught in a high wind. She shuddered and shivered and moaned with stark delight when he raced back into her.

Slocum started moving faster and faster. The heat mounted along his length until he felt as if he would explode at any instant like a young buck on his first ride. He gripped down harder on Maude's meaty rump, pulled her forcefully into him and ground his crotch against hers until they were both moaning with pleasure.

"More, John, more. Fast. Hard. I want it all!"

He gave it to her. Looking down at her passion-racked face spurred him on to move with more speed and power. He buried himself repeatedly into her yearning interior until he felt a powerful contraction all around his length. Slocum kept moving, the friction mounting until he was sure he would be burned to a nub.

And still he moved, trying to hold back the fiery tide that threatened to explode at any instant from within. He knew Maude was responding. He felt her jerk and tremble as the erotic earthquake rattled through her trim young physique. Then Slocum could not withstand the onslaught of her beauty and body. An especially intense tensing around his buried manstalk set him off.

He grunted, arched his back and rammed forward hard, trying to split her apart. She twisted and turned and thrashed about beneath him until they were both spent. Slocum sagged forward and then flopped on his side on the bed.

"Don't want to get blood on your bedspread," he said,

lying on his right side so he could look the woman squarely in the eye. Her chocolate-colored eyes danced with lust—still.

"Right now, I don't much care what happens to the bedspread," she told him. "We've already wrinkled and stained it, and I say hurrah!"

She snuggled closer to him, her breasts warm against his chest. Maude lifted a leg and draped it across his thigh and moved even closer.

"Gets mighty cold in Idaho this time of year," she said by way of explanation. Slocum wasn't complaining.

"How come a pretty filly like you doesn't have a steady fellow?" Slocum asked.

Maude laughed softly. "I used to but a fever took him from me."

"Cholera?"

She laughed again, this time more bitterly. "No, it was gold fever. He decided it was better digging in the cold ground for gold than it was lying beside me in a warm bed."

"He was a fool," Slocum said.

"You think so?"

"Yes."

"Don't go saying things you don't believe, John Slocum. I know your type. You're just like Cray. No woman ties you down, not for long. Especially a saloon keeper like me."

Slocum didn't answer because Maude was right. As pretty as she was, as intriguing and as good in bed, that wasn't enough to keep him from hunting for what was just over the horizon or on top of the next mountain.

"Why'd Sheriff Pennant bust up your place? From what you and Sid said, this isn't the first time."

"The sheriff's got a wild hair up his ass," Maude said. "He's a rabid prohibitionist. Or maybe he's just rabid. You haven't been in Woodchip long enough to notice, but the Fancy Lady is the only saloon left. Pennant's chased out everyone else because most of the townsfolk are Mormons and don't believe in boozing it up. Can't say anything against their religion, but they make it hard for someone like me to earn a decent living from those people around town who appreciate a snort or two to ease the pain and loneliness."

"Why haven't you pulled up stakes and moved on? From what you say, you don't have anything keeping you here."

"Stubborn," Maude said. "I'm so downright stubborn it'll be the death of me. The sheriff's not going to run me off, even if he has the power of the law on his side."

"It's illegal to sell whiskey in Woodchip?" This startled Slocum. With the lumberjacks all around town, with a few gold mines dotting the mountains, with the folks in town all working up a powerful thirst, he couldn't imagine them going along with any law against peddling rotgut.

"Not exactly. The sheriff enforces laws that don't—quite—exist. Call them moral tenets rather than wrote-down laws. That might be one reason I stay on. He has no right to come in and destroy my whiskey, but he does anyway."

"Why don't you get some of the lumberjacks to stop him?"

"You think they'd risk their necks over a shot or two of booze? Hardly. All those woodenheads want is a shot of whiskey followed by a fistfight."

Slocum thought Maude misjudged the men around Woodchip. She could talk a bird down from a tree if she put her mind to it. More than one man might just stand up to the sheriff if she asked politely. Even the Mormon citizens might be amenable to her keeping the Fancy Lady out of their town but letting it operate if it was out of sight, down the road a piece toward Coeur d'Alene.

"Might be I can do something to help out," Slocum said.

"That six-shooter of yours has a well-used look to it," Maude said carefully. "But that's not all that's been well-used." She rubbed her crotch against his upper thigh as she reached down to find his flaccid manhood.

"See? You can talk me into anything," Slocum said, feeling himself beginning to respond again.

Maude laughed, this time with real amusement. "You don't think with *this*." She gave him a tweak that got him even harder. "There's too much going on in your head, John, for *this* to run your life."

"Maybe so, but I can offer to help out a friend, can't I?"

"We're friends?" She started kissing at his chest.

"Good friends," Slocum said. "But I was thinking of a business deal."

Maude recoiled and looked up at him. Slocum couldn't read her ever-changing expression. It flowed from disbelief to horror.

"Business? That the way you want it?"

"Not this," he said, reaching down and catching her wrist to hold her hand in place. "I'll see what I can do to get the sheriff to see the error of his ways if you can help me find Randall Claymore. Do you know him?"

"Heard the name but don't know him by sight."

"He was the one who tried to rob Finch when he left the saloon."

"You're going after Claymore because he tried to rob Finch? I don't believe that. You didn't know the Britisher from Adam before this afternoon."

"I was hunting Claymore for other reasons. Not to kill him," Slocum explained quickly, but he knew it might come to that if he found that Claymore had been the one who ambushed him out on the road.

"So, if I ask around about Claymore, you'll ask Pennant to stop pestering me?"

"Something like that," Slocum said.

"And none of that has anything to do with *this*?" She began running her teasing, tormenting fingers up and down his hardened pillar.

"Nothing," Slocum said, grinning. "And it certainly has nothing to do with this." He rolled atop her. Maude's legs spread wantonly for him as he probed once again to find the spot they both wanted filled.

It took the rest of the night to consummate their deal.

4

"You run along now," Maude told Slocum. She stood with her hands on her flaring hips, staring at the mess in the saloon. "I'll get that good-for-nothing Sid in here and clean up this mess."

"What are you going to do then? Do you want me to guard a shipment of whiskey from Coeur d'Alene?"

"Not right now. I'll start easy and irritate Pennant by serving food and water straight out of the rain barrel. When he gets good and prickly, then I'll think about bringing in more whiskey."

"You're a lightning rod for trouble," Slocum said, shaking his head.

"Look who's talking. Get on out of here, 'fore I hand you a broom and make you sweep up the debris."

Slocum started to move the chair holding the door in place when he heard Maude coming up behind him. He hesitated and half turned to find the woman in his arms.

"You didn't think I'd let you go without saying a proper good-bye, did you?" She planted a big kiss on his lips. "Now get on out of here. I have work to do."

"Don't forget to ask after Randall Claymore," Slocum said, wrestling the chair aside in time to catch the falling door. He leaned it against the wall and stepped out into Woodchip's main street.

He stretched and felt the skin on his back protest a mite. Maude had patched him up pretty good, bandaging his wound expertly. The rest of her medicine had done him even more good.

Slocum turned toward the stables to see to his horse. He slipped into the stables through a side door and heard a peculiar noise. Drawing his six-gun, he went to see what made the sound. Slocum returned his pistol to his holster when he saw Finch still sprawled where he had left him the night before.

Finch stirred, grumbled and then sat bolt upright, eyes wide and staring at Slocum.

"You startled me, old man." Finch looked around and frowned, wondering how he had come to be in the stables.

"I made sure you were all right last night," Slocum said. His wound gave him a twinge, but he said nothing about it to Finch. Wearing a discarded shirt Maude had found hid the wound entirely.

"You are a prince among men. Allow me to thank you by buying you breakfast."

"I'm headed out of town," Slocum said. "You know where I might find Claymore?"

"Claymore? Ah, yes the brigand who tried to rob me. What a foolish thing to do. You can't steal from a poor man."

"How're you going to buy me breakfast if you're so poor?" asked Slocum, grinning. He knew the answer before Finch said anything. Finch would have taken him to the town's café but would have stuck him with the check.

"I am known locally," Finch said proudly. "Miz Hawkins at the quaint café allows me to charge my meals until the first of every month."

"Your remittance comes then?" asked Slocum.

"Ah, news travels so fast in small towns," Finch said

with some sadness. "I had hoped to deceive you into thinking I was a man of independent means."

"What brought you to Idaho?" asked Slocum, saddling his horse and getting ready to find Claymore.

"Chance, greed, both of those demons. Whether I chased them or they chased me, who is to say?" Finch brushed himself off. "I am the proud owner of a major cattle ranch."

"What's that?" Slocum thought he had misheard the Britisher. "You own a spread?"

"I do, more's the pity. Would you like to see my contribution to the legends of the West?"

"All right," Slocum said, thinking he had to ride in some direction and he might find out more about Randall Claymore if he rode with Finch.

They rode out of town, heading in the direction Claymore had run the night before after trying to rob Finch.

"How'd you come to be a rancher?" Slocum asked.

"I was languishing in Denver, at loose ends and not sure what to do with myself when I met Justin Dunlop. He struck me as a bonny fellow, well liked in his social circle and of some means."

"He was a fraud who sold you worthless land," Slocum finished, knowing he might listen to Finch the rest of the day unless he cut through to the bone.

"More than that. The land is rocky and struggles to grow weeds, much less the fine, succulent grasses favored by bulky cattle. He also sold me the stock for the ranch. I thought so highly of him, I accepted his word and purchased it sight unseen."

"Is that one?" Slocum pointed to a skeletal cow stumbling along to find any patch of grass it could.

"If it's not, it could be," Finch said tiredly. "Truth to tell, that might count as a superior bovine among my herd. Breeding has proven difficult, also, since Dunlop did not include a bull among the scrawny herd. Perhaps that is just as well. I don't think I could bear up under the rattling of bones all night long."

In spite of himself, Slocum had to laugh.

"I'm glad you see the humor in it," Slocum said.

"One either laughs or cries. I have done my share of the latter. Ah, there, Mr. Slocum, there is my palace on the prairie."

Slocum started to point out this was no prairie, not with mountains rising up all around, but fell silent when he saw the house.

"Looks adequate," Slocum said. "I've seen worse. In fact, I've lived in worse." He rode to the front porch, dismounted and took the steps two at a time to the front door.

"Go on," Finch said. "Look around my luxurious chateau."

Slocum opened the door and peered into the dusty interior. He quickly closed it when a loud snarl echoed inside. Something big and gray had made a den inside, something with sharp teeth and a tendency to protect its cubs.

"You can get the wolves out," Slocum said, looking for the hole where the she-wolf came and went from the house. Wolves were smart but not smart enough to open and close a latched door.

"I could, yes," agreed Finch. "To what purpose? The cattle are all falling down and on the verge of death. I cannot tell if it is disease or simple starvation."

"What do you know about ranching?" Slocum asked. The expression on Finch's face told him the answer: The man knew nothing at all. "Why'd you buy this place?"

"I did so because that is the way fortunes are made out West," Finch said. "Dunlop was such an open, trustworthy sort of bloke."

"And you don't know anything about cattle?"

"I enjoy a good porterhouse steak," Finch said.

Slocum saw that wasn't all Finch enjoyed. The man reached into an inner pocket of his fancy coat and drew out a silver flask. A quick snort from it put him back into a good humor. Finch hesitated, whiskey flask in hand, torn between keeping the precious liquor for himself and offering Slocum a drink.

"No, thanks," Slocum said, before Finch could work up his courage to do one or the other. For Slocum it was too early in the day to partake.

Finch looked relieved and tucked away the flask. He strutted about, then turned and looked up at where Slocum stood on the porch.

"You seem a sturdy man of the West," Finch said. "Do you know anything about cattle growing and running a vast ranch such as the Rolling J?"

"That's what you call this spread?"

"That was the name given it by Dunlop. I suppose since he took my money, I can take the name. Frankly, I can't think of another to give it, being something of a neophyte at such things."

"If the rest of your herd looks like that cow down by the road, there's nothing I can do to help," Slocum said. "Short of butchering the entire herd, there's nothing anybody can do."

"I feared as much." Finch let out a gusty sigh, then reached for his flask again.

"Have you looked over the entire spread? Is it all as rocky as this part?"

"I have not come farther than this house and its immediate environs, Mr. Slocum. There seemed no good reason to expend the effort."

"Ride the fences, see what you've actually bought. There might be better grazing land in that direction." Slocum pointed toward the mountains. "It's rocky here but might turn to meadowlands at a higher altitude."

"That would be a more scenic location for my house,"

Finch said, "but unless there is some vast stretch of mountain loveliness, it won't be enough for a large herd of cattle."

"Might be you can start small and learn the trade," Slocum suggested.

"That sounds so much like work," Finch said, knocking back another shot from his flask.

"There's nothing you can substitute for hard work," Slocum said. He glanced up at the sun pushing its way toward midheaven and knew he had spent enough time with Finch. He had to find Randall Claymore.

"That is a bugaboo that will return to haunt me," Finch said.

"You knew Claymore. Where'd you come across him before?" asked Slocum. When he saw Finch's momentary incomprehension, he added, "The man who tried to rob you." The tarantula juice Finch swilled constantly was beginning to cloud his brain.

"Ah, that brigand, yes. I met him at another saloon in Woodchip, when there was another besides the Fancy Lady. We spoke, traded lies, bought each other a drink or two. I thought nothing of it, that he was only being neighborly."

" 'Neighborly?' " Slocum pounced on it. "Does that mean Claymore lives around here? I'd heard tell he was a prospector or a gold miner. Is he somewhere up in the hills?"

"I don't know about his noble quest for gold," Finch said, starting to slur his words now. "What I meant to say is that he's got a place out by Whiskey Lake."

"Where I found you yesterday?"

"Yes," Finch said, sinking down to sit on a large rock.

"What were you doing there? Looking for Claymore?"

"Why ever would I do that? I hardly know the bloke. I was looking for . . . something else." The way Finch's words trailed off told Slocum he had gotten all the answers he was likely to right now.

"If I cut across your land, go over those hills yonder and head south, would that bring me to Whiskey Lake?"

Finch looked confused. "Ride about my spread all you like, Mr. Slocum. Take it all in!" Finch threw up his hands and tumbled backward onto the ground. He quickly picked himself up, hiccuped and reached for his flask again.

"Thanks," Slocum said. "Will you be all right?" He glanced over his shoulder in the direction of the ranch house filled with its snarling she-wolf and cubs.

"I will, sir," Finch said with drunken dignity. "I know better than to disturb nature." He pointed at the front door.

Slocum reluctantly left the Britisher, but Finch wouldn't be any help finding Randall Claymore in his condition. Slocum set out in what he reckoned to be a straight line that would take him over a ridge to the southeast, then lead down to the shore of Whiskey Lake.

He kept a sharp eye out for cattle but saw few. All were in the same condition as the one he and Finch had seen riding up to the Rolling J ranch house. But the land was nowhere as rocky in this direction, and Slocum thought there might be decent patches for grazing a small herd. Whether it would pay to raise only a few dozen head of cattle was something else. The entire region was caught up in a logging and mining boom right now, and Slocum thought Finch could sell all the cattle he could raise.

A few dozen cattle might be better than nothing, if the man wanted to work at it. From everything Slocum had seen, though, that would be a big hurdle for Finch to overcome. The man was a ne'er-do-well and had probably never done a real day's work in his life.

After riding most of the afternoon, Slocum reached the top of the ridge looking down on Whiskey Lake. The water looked appealing, shining like liquid silver in the late day's sunlight. Slocum dismounted, took out a pair of binoculars he had won off a cavalry officer in a poker game a few months earlier and slowly scanned the land around the lake for any sign of Randall Claymore.

Not only didn't he spot Claymore, he saw no trace of anyone along the lakefront.

Slocum found the area agreeable and settled down to watch the lake and any activity around it, but found himself growing restive after an hour or so. The sun was sinking, and he had not spotted a single soul anywhere near the lake. He considered riding around the perimeter of the lake hunting for loggers or prospectors who might know Claymore. Finch had been damnably vague about where the inept robber might be found.

Pulling himself into the saddle, Slocum felt a momentary twinge in his back, and then it went away. Maude had done a right good job fixing him up—and he didn't mean with the bandaging. Her kind of medicine had made him feel better than he had at any time since leaving Kansas.

Guiding the Appaloosa downhill in the gathering gloom, Slocum finally found the meager road that led past the lake. He considered starting out right away but had the feeling of being watched. Try as he might, he couldn't find anyone studying him as he had studied Whiskey Lake all afternoon. He shrugged it off as nerves, but deep down he trusted his instinct more than that.

Slocum rode from the lake, heading back to the road leading into Woodchip. He hoped to find sign of riders; possibly the gang that had ambushed him had come this way. Unsure what he was looking for or what he would find, he wasn't too surprised when he heard the distant crack of a rifle, followed quickly buy the deep-throated roar of a shotgun discharging. Several other shots echoed along the road. All came from pistols.

With such a battle going on, Slocum had to figure the

road agents were hard at work and somebody law abiding needed his help.

Galloping toward the gunfire, Slocum reached down and drew the Winchester from its sheath. He cocked it and got ready for the fight to come when he topped a rise and saw a fork in the road. One branch led to Woodchip. The other came down from Coeur d'Alene. A hundred yards along the Coeur d'Alene road he saw a half dozen highwaymen, bandannas pulled up over their faces, shooting at three freighters. The freighters had abandoned their wagons and had taken cover behind rocks and fallen trees near the road.

Slocum waved and got the attention of one freighter. The man signalled that Slocum ought to hit the road agents from the rear. He considered his best approach, then decided stealth wasn't as good an ally as convincing the robbers they had been caught by an entire posse.

Whooping and hollering, Slocum began firing both his rifle and Colt Navy to cause as big a ruckus as possible.

As with everything else that had gone on since he had reached Idaho, he found himself flabbergasted at how others reacted. The brigands divided their fire between him and the freighters, but three of them rushed to the wagons and began hacking away at the cargo with axes.

Spray went up as the three masked men worked and then the others joined them with their horses so they could race off into the gathering twilight.

Slocum started after them, firing until his rifle magazine came up empty. He shoved his Colt back into the holster because he had long since fired all six rounds.

"You gents still in one piece?" he called, not wanting the freighters to mistake him for one of the robbers.

"Thanks to you, we are," said the one who had signalled Slocum to attack. "I'd offer you some of our cargo, but it don't look like we got none left."

Slocum took a deep breath and found himself filling his lungs with a familiar odor. Whiskey.

"You taking that to the Fancy Lady Saloon?" Slocum asked.

"We were," the freighter said. "Them varmints smashed most of the barrels. We got a few left but not many. Here, come on over here and help yourself, if you don't mind the likker bein' strained through the bottom of my wagon."

Slocum filled his almost empty canteen with the whiskey dripping from the wagon. The casks it had been shipped in were wood. It didn't make much difference to him if the whiskey was poured over another plank or two on its way to his lips.

"We were bringin' the load down from Coeur d'Alene," the freighter said, "when them owlhoots jumped us. Dangest thing. It was like they wanted to destroy the whiskey rather than rob us."

"Don't suppose you noticed if any of them wore badges?" Slocum asked.

"How's that, mister? I don't understand."

"I don't, either," Slocum said, slowly sipping at the dregs of the rye whiskey, "but I aim to."

5

"It came, Mr. Slocum, it came!" James Barrington-Finch did a jig in the middle of the street, holding a letter high over his head.

"The mail brought you something you were waiting for," Slocum said, guessing what caused Finch's good humor. It was the first of the month and time for the man's money to arrive.

"The bank in St. Louis is most precise about delivering my remittance with alacrity," Finch said. "I am, until I spend this fine amount of money, rich again!" Laughing the man headed toward the far end of town. Slocum called after him, asking where he was going but Finch was too lost in his own joy to hear.

"He's going to start paying his bills," Maude said, coming up behind Slocum. He noticed how she brushed against him. Nothing overt to cause gossip among the strict citizens of Woodchip, but enough to let him know she appreciated how they had spent the night. Slocum felt a mite guilty about the time he had spent over the past week in Woodchip rather than hunting for Randall Claymore, but Maude was a powerful inducement not to stray too far.

"What's he do, go to one end of town and pay off everyone along the way?"

"Something like that," Maude said. "Depending on his mood, he starts at the north end and works south or sometimes the other way."

"Don't the people at the opposite end of town worry? Finch has rolled up considerable bills."

"He owes me danged near a hundred dollars," Maude said, "but he is good for it. His remittance is ample. I wish mine was." She looked down at her bosoms, then glanced sideways at Slocum.

He grinned. "Quit fishing for compliments. You are more than ample."

"You'd say that because you have big hands. I feel so small when you—" Maude bit off her whispered comment about where Slocum had placed his hands when Finch came swinging back, whistling a jaunty tune.

"Ah, my favorite people in all of Woodchip!" he greeted Maude and Slocum. "I have paid my due to the delightful merchants and still have money left."

"You haven't paid me," Maude pointed out.

"I shall, my dear Maude, I shall. What sort of shindig, I think you Yanks call it, can I throw for two hundred dollars?"

"You owe me a hundred on your tab, so you'd have a full hundred left over," Maude said.

"I want only the finest viands," Finch said grandly. To Slocum he said, "That means food, sir."

"I know. You can get food but whiskey would be hard, considering the way Sheriff Pennant looks down his nose at it."

"Ah, the good sheriff, yes," Finch said, as if the lawman was only a small obstacle to overcome. "He has declared a holy war, so to speak, but surely I can speak with him about turning the other cheek, looking the other way, if only for a solitary night. I feel the need to *celebrate*!"

Slocum started to point out that the money Finch would spend on his rowdy party would go a ways toward buying breeding stock for the ranch but he held his tongue. It was Finch's money, or at least his father's, and he could spend it as he saw fit. This way Maude benefitted, so it wasn't all going to waste.

"You can see why they dole it out to him, a little bit every month," Maude said, not caring that Finch heard her comment to Slocum.

"I have no willpower," Finch admitted. "And I certainly have a powerful taste for the spirits. Do what you can. I need to invite a few select friends to the bash."

Finch went off, whistling his tune and greeting people in the street. From what Slocum could tell, Finch was inviting anyone who so much as said "Howdy" to him.

"We'll have every no-account, hollow-legged, sex-starved, parched-throated lumberjack within twenty miles at the Fancy Lady tonight," Maude said with some relish. "I've got to convince Sid to stay on, at least until tomorrow when there'll be a powerful lot of cleaning up to do."

Slocum had to laugh. From what Maude said, Sid quit at least twice a week but always stayed, sometimes reluctantly, sometimes because Maude cajoled him and always because she promised him more money. If Maude was right and she gave him a raise every time he threatened to walk out, he must be making as much as Finch every month.

Slocum reckoned the number was a lot less and that Sid stayed because of devotion to Maude.

"How are you going to get the whiskey?"

"You saved a bit of my shipment from Coeur d'Alene," Maude said, "but I've been rationing it out to select customers this past week, and there's not much left. I'll need at least a barrel, and maybe three, for Finch's jubilee."

"It won't matter if you have enough to float Finch's tonsils, if the sheriff shuts you down. Finch will lose his money and Pennant might toss you in the hoosegow."

"He wouldn't dare," Maude said hotly. "He's a coward. He couldn't handle the trouble he'd be in if he tried."

"He's got the law on his side if he got the mayor and aldermen to agree to his no-drinking ordinance."

"Major Jackson and the rest are scared of their own shadows," Maude declared. "I could talk rings around them. They might not permit drinking among their own, but you'd be surprised what goes on privately. Woodchip is a long ways from Salt Lake City and the center of their religious influence."

"So if Pennant shouts 'jump,' the mayor and the city council ask how high?"

"Something like that, but only if he gets to them before I do."

"You go right to the heart of your trouble," Slocum said, shaking his head. "You don't fool around with men like that, because they either can't or won't make decisions."

"What are you saying, John?" Maude looked at him with new respect. She knew what he was suggesting.

"I'll have a talk with the sheriff to see if there's not some way around his town ordinance."

"Every man has his price, right?" Maude asked. She turned and faced him, looking up into his green eyes. "What's your price, John?"

"Money isn't everything," he said.

"I never mentioned money. What's your price?"

"Let me go find Finch," Slocum said.

"And I need to get the Fancy Lady fixed up so my customers can destroy it again. I just don't want the sheriff being the one smashing windows and chairs. He and his thumb-fingered deputies do a better job than any drunk."

Slocum's long strides covered the ground between him and Finch. Finch was paying off a bill at the general store and had just accepted an apple for his prompt payment. He tossed it to Slocum.

"All yours, my good man. I try not to pollute my body with such things." Finch let out a deep sigh. "How I wish I could find a decent supply of marmalade, though. I do so miss it with my biscuits at tea."

Slocum polished the apple on his jacket and bit into it. The sweet juices were as good as any whiskey, but he knew better than to try to convince Finch of that. A man with a taste for bourbon and rye wasn't likely to like much else.

"You're putting a lot on Maude's shoulders," Slocum said.

"How's that?"

"Sheriff Pennant isn't likely to let any party get started if there's whiskey flowing."

"Ah, I see your point. You are suggesting that I approach the lawless lawman in arbitration over the shindig?"

"It might be interesting to see what Pennant says."

"From your tone, Mr. Slocum, you think I can be successful in bribing him into permitting the party."

"I can't argue with that," Slocum said, because it was exactly what he thought. Dangle enough money in front of Pennant's nose and all his objections to liquor would vanish. Slocum hadn't figured out exactly what Pennant had to gain driving out all the saloons but the way he reacted to Finch's proposal would go a ways toward explaining it. Religious beliefs might be responsible, but Slocum's gut told him different.

"Do you wish to come along?" asked Finch.

"Don't mind if I do, but I'll hang back so you two can talk in private. This isn't something the sheriff is likely to spread around town."

"Ah, yes, the forbidden fruit being all the sweeter," Finch said. "If anyone overhears, it might no longer be possible to barter because of his high public office."

Slocum scratched his head, then worked on the apple as he trailed behind Finch. They found Sheriff Pennant at the end of town away from the Fancy Lady, sitting under a tree, his broad-brimmed hat tipped down over his eyes as he caught a few winks.

"A gracious good morning, Sheriff," boomed Finch. The lawman jerked erect, his hand going for his six-shooter. When he saw he wasn't being threatened he growled deep in his throat like a fierce dog and glared at Finch.

"Whatya want, limey?"

"Why, I have a proposition for you."

Finch hunkered down and began talking in a low voice while Slocum watched from a distance. He knew what Finch said and had no need to see the man's face. He watched Pennant like a hawk as the bribe was being offered. Pennant's expression changed from one of outrage to downright greed, as Slocum had suspected. The sheriff's opposition to liquor served in Woodchip apparently could be dulled like a cheap knife if enough money was forked over.

A few minutes later, Finch came back and he and Slocum walked down the center of the street in the direction of the Fancy Lady.

"That was quite revealing," Finch said. "I had suspected some small argument, but when I offered twenty dollars, he positively leapt at it."

"That's all?" Slocum raised an eyebrow. It was far less than he had expected Pennant to take. "He didn't even dicker with you?"

"Not a bit of it, old chap. Well, I must see to my guest list. You, of course, are to be a guest of honor this evening. Sundown till dawn! Toodle-oo!" With that cheery parting, Finch rushed off to invite others to his party. Slocum walked more slowly now, finished his apple and tossed the core down an alley toward a pile of garbage.

He wiped his mouth as he entered the Fancy Lady, thinking hard about the sheriff and how quickly he had been bought.

"What's the good word, Slocum?" asked Sid. "You have the look of someone who's figured it all out."

"I just need to find what 'it' is," he told Sid. "Where's Maude?"

"She, uh, she took off. Business."

"Finch got the sheriff to agree to look the other way tonight. All you need now is some whiskey." Slocum saw the barkeep's expression and guessed where Maude had gone. There had to be more than one source for booze in the area. The shipment from Coeur d'Alene showed that the bigger sellers could move a dozen barrels at a time. Another source had to be closer to Woodchip or Maude wouldn't be gone right now.

"I'll be ready. There's good money to be had from that gent," Sid said with some glee.

"See you then," Slocum said. He stepped back out into the chilly morning sun and looked around the town. Some signs of commerce built, people coming and going from the shops, but Slocum wanted to find Maude. He set off down the street, heading south for no good reason other than it felt right to him.

At the end of the buildings, where the trees came right up to the road, Slocum spotted the woman hurrying along. He started to call out to her but held back, curious to see where she was going. For all the time they had spent together, he still knew next to nothing about her.

A wry smile came to his lips as that thought crossed his mind. He played his cards close to the vest, too. That was the way people kept from getting hurt, but it did nothing to help him understand her—or to find Randall Claymore. She had said she would ask around about Claymore, and Maude might have, but Slocum had not come any closer to getting the papers signed than when he had ridden into Woodchip.

Maude suddenly left the road and plunged into a thicket. Slocum trailed her into the woods, moving as softly as a shadow. The woman made no effort to hide where she went, crashing through bushes and breaking low limbs on saplings. She began cursing as she went but didn't slow her determined progress. That made Slocum even more curious about whom she went to meet.

"Help me, dammit!" Maude called. For a second, Slocum thought she had spotted him and was calling for aid. Then he saw a small, dark figure flitting through the forest.

"You got caught on the thornbush," the other man growled as he pulled Maude's dress free.

"I tore it. It'll take me all day to patch my dress."

"You got the money?" the man demanded.

Slocum slipped through the woods and found a thick-boled pine tree to hide behind. He peered around the tree and saw Maude fussing over the tear in her dress. Next to her, hardly taller than the short woman, a man with an irritated expression glared at her.

"Well?" he asked.

"I have it, I have it," Maude said, still more concerned about her dress. "When will you deliver the rotgut?"

"After dark. Don't dare move more'n two barrels when the sheriff kin see me."

"Then bring it to the rear of the Fancy Lady around seven. I think I have enough from my other supplier to keep things roaring until then." Maude fumbled in a pocket hidden away in her skirts and pulled out a roll of greenbacks. She jerked away from the man when he grabbed for them.

"Gimme!"

"Not so fast, Ethan," she said. "Try that again and I'll bust your damned wrist."

Slocum saw that Ethan didn't like being scolded by Maude but was willing to put up with it for the sake of the money she counted out slowly. When she tucked away what was left of her bankroll, she held out his money. Ethan grabbed for it again, like a hawk swooping down on a field mouse.

"You'd better deliver, and don't worry about the sheriff. That's been taken care of," Maude said.

"What do you mean?" Ethan clutched the money and stared suspiciously at Maude.

"Finch is throwing this party tonight, and he paid off the sheriff."

"Pennant'll look the other way?"

"That's what Finch says, and he knows about such things."

Slocum was interested in Ethan's reaction. The man showed a flash of anger that faded as fast as it appeared.

"Two barrels of my best. You'll get it tonight, Maude."

The saloon owner said nothing more, turning and retracing her path through the woods. Slocum started after her, then stopped. It would satisfy his curiosity more finding where the moonshiner went.

Slocum tried to pick up Ethan's tracks but the man, whether out of habit or because he worried someone might follow him, did all he could to hide his tracks. Slocum was a good tracker but lost Ethan when the man waded into a stream. If he had wanted, Slocum could have found where the moonshiner left by carefully going up and down the creek and hunting for tracks. It hardly seemed worth it since he knew where Ethan was going to be at seven o'clock that night. He wasn't sure Ethan and his moonshining were worth his time, but he could pursue the matter later if his curiosity was still piqued.

Slocum returned to Woodchip to sit around, keeping his ears open and his eyes peeled for any trace of Randall Claymore.

6

Slocum sat at a lopsided table to one side of the main room, watching everyone who entered the Fancy Lady, in the hope of spotting Randall Claymore. He doubted the man would be stupid enough to try to rob a man then come to a revel paid for by his intended victim. Still, Slocum had heard of dumber things, and didn't want to take any chances.

He couldn't keep himself from smiling when he saw Maude across the room. Her lovely, soft, brunette hair seemed to float like ocean mist and then vanish amid the sea of lumberjacks and miners. She moved easily between the men, always avoiding their clumsy attempts to paw her and never losing her good nature. Maude was in her element here, one that Slocum could never fully appreciate. He hankered for a drink of whiskey now and then the same as any man, but he could never put up for very long with this many people crowding all around him. It made him a little antsy as it was, sitting to one side of the room, his back to a corner.

Wild Bill Hickok notwithstanding, Slocum never felt comfortable exposing his back to a roomful of rowdies. He didn't fear any of them, and for the first time in ages no one was actively chasing him. While he had more than a few wanted posters drifting around the West with his likeness gracing them, Slocum doubted any had landed on Sheriff Pennant's desk.

The uneasiness he had grew like Topsy from too many bodies crammed into too small a space and nothing more.

"Beer!" Finch cried in disbelief. The Britisher jumped to a table and wobbled about, supported by a few of the men below him. Slocum wondered how much Finch had drunk before this shindig had even started. "What's going on, Maude! Where's the real stuff? The whiskey?"

"It's being delivered soon enough, Finch," Maude called. "If you get any drunker, you won't be able to swill it when it does get here!"

"Ah, my dear, you are *so* wrong! I can drink all night long and still sing with the mourning doves come sunup!"

Finch let out a cry of glee, then dived off the table, trusting that the men under him would grab him. They didn't and he smashed hard into the floorboards. Slocum half rose to go to the man's aid, then saw Finch was already so drunk he hardly noticed.

"Dance! Let's dance!" Finch cried. The few women in the room began to swing and sway through the crowd while Maude spoke over the bar to Sid. The barkeep kept shaking his head and pointing to the rear door. Slocum didn't have to read their lips to know that Maude wasn't happy that the bootleg whiskey hadn't been delivered yet.

He went to the newly repaired front door and looked outside. Across the street, looking glum, loitered Sheriff Pennant's two deputies. The sheriff himself was nowhere to be seen. Slocum almost called out an invitation for them to join the party, then decided that wasn't too good an idea. The sheriff might not like whiskey being served in town, but he was crooked enough to take a bribe to look the other way. He might be unprincipled enough to blame Finch's partying on the two deputies if they put in an appearance.

Other than the two lawmen, Woodchip's main street was as empty as a whore's heart.

Slocum turned back in time to see both Maude and Sid duck out the back. He left the front way, circled the rickety building and got to the side of the saloon in time to see a man jump from a buckboard.

"It's about time you got here, Ethan," Maude said angrily. "You told me you'd deliver the whiskey an hour ago."

"Got held up. Pennant's deputies rousted me when I was loadin' the likker. I had to give them an extra ten dollars each to look the other way."

"When might that have been?" Slocum asked, coming up. Ethan's hand flashed for his belt. He froze when he saw Slocum already had his Colt Navy out and pointed at his gut.

"On my way here," Ethan said. "And who the hell are you?"

"What's wrong, John?" Maude asked.

"The two deputies have been across the street for over an hour. Reckon I should go ask them why they're taking bribes and not passing it along to the sheriff?" Slocum watched Ethan closely. The man paled under the dirt on his face. A grimy hand swiped across his mouth and then Ethan began shaking his head.

"That won't be necessary. I ain't gonna make you pay the bribe, Maude. Just wanted you to know why I was late, that's all."

"Get the barrels unloaded," Maude said, flashing a smile of thanks in Slocum's direction. She knew he had just saved her from Ethan's shakedown for more money.

Sid and Ethan grunted as they struggled to get the heavy casks out of the rear of the buckboard.

"You want to join the fun?" Maude asked Ethan.

"Got work to do," the man said sullenly, glaring at Slocum.

"That'll save you a quart or two of tarantula juice," Slocum said as they watched Ethan drive off, grumbling to himself.

"You saved me having to pay him more, too. It's a good thing you're around, John. You're saving me money *and* showing you can be useful in other ways, too."

"I'll show you how useful. Later," he promised.

Maude laughed delightedly and went in the rear door. Slocum helped Sid roll the second barrel into the storeroom and wrestle the other out into the saloon. A cheer went up when Sid knocked out a bung and drove in a spigot to begin dispensing whiskey.

Slocum sampled the witchy brew. If he had half a mind to get soused, this would have been perfect. The liquor had a bite like a grizzly to it, then delivered the kick of a mule to the gut after it had settled. Maude definitely got her money's worth with the two barrels.

He had to wonder how much of the moonshine whiskey ended up going down Finch's throat. Sometime after two in the morning, the Britisher had drunk most of the loggers under the table. The prospectors had passed out before midnight.

"Whass wrong wit' ever'buddy?" Finch demanded. "You all stoppin' drinkin' early? Don'tcha like me?"

"You're a prince of a fellow, Finch," Maude said, "but you're partying all by yourself. The rest have passed out."

"Damn Yanks," he grumbled. "Never can, could, they can't hold their liquor."

Finch half turned and collapsed into Slocum's arms.

"Go on, John, get him home. Neither of us in much condition to keep celebrating," Maude said.

Slocum had drunk very little, and he doubted Maude had imbibed any more than he had, but he knew what she meant. Finch had paid for this jubilee and deserved to be escorted home safely.

"Come on," Slocum said, dragging Finch with him. "Let's get you out to your ranch."

"Thanks, John. *You're* a prince," Maude said. She stood on tiptoe and kissed him quickly.

Slocum struggled to get Finch outside and onto a horse. He considered letting him sleep off his drunk in the stables as he apparently did often, then figured he owed it to the man to be sure he had a decent spot to sleep.

The ride out to Finch's Rolling J Ranch went quickly enough, though the rising wind turned the Idaho night into one approaching winter. Slocum considered going into the house and seeing if the she-wolf still had her den there. More than once, Slocum had seen a wolf move her cubs when too many men came snooping by. That might have happened this time, but he was too tired to risk the wolf waiting inside the door, fangs bared and ready to snap off his leg.

"Come on out to the barn," Slocum said, wondering what ferocious creatures might have taken up residence there. To his surprise, the barn was well maintained, considering the entire ranch obviously had been deserted for so long before Finch bought it. He dropped Finch into a stall, then got his own bedroll and found another stall.

Slocum spread out his blanket, rolled onto his side and was asleep in minutes. He came awake when sunlight slanted through a broken board and fell across his face. Stretching, he sat up and looked around. His initial impression was right. The barn was in good condition.

Finch still slept off his drunk in the next stall, so Slocum went exploring. He took his rifle along when he went into the house. To his relief, the wolf had abandoned this risky human dwelling in favor of a cave or hollow somewhere out in the woods. Resting the rifle against one wall, Slocum found a broom and began sweeping and cleaning, getting the house into a more presentable condition.

He had been working about an hour, making a mental list of chores that had to be done, not the least of which was repairing the roof. From the way the sun came through a dozen holes, anyone inside would get wetter than if they were outside in a driving rain, should one of the fierce Idaho storms come sweeping through from Canada.

As he poked at the roof with the broom handle to test its substance, Slocum heard the steady thudding of hoofbeats. He put down the broom and moved the rifle so it was just inside the door as he opened it to see a half dozen lumberjacks.

"Howdy, mister! You the new owner of this here spread?" called a burly lumberjack on a horse half again the size of Slocum's Appaloosa. It had to be that big to support the man's weight.

"You boys work around here?" Slocum asked.

"About a mile on the other side of that fence, if you can call it a fence," said the big logger, laughing. "We're 'jacks for the Pacific Northern Timber Company."

"What can I do for you?" Slocum didn't think he would need the rifle. The loggers had knives at their belts but no six-shooters. From their genial attitudes, he had nothing to fear from them.

"Water, sir," spoke up another logger. "We were in town last night at 'bout the biggest drunken orgy I ever seen."

"In Woodchip? I was there, too."

"Naw, you couldna been. You don't look hungover," protested the biggest of the lumberjacks.

"What's going on?" asked Finch, stumbling down from the barn and looking at the mounted men through half-slitted eyelids.

"These fellows want some water from the well. Is the water good?" asked Slocum.

"It certainly is. The finest water this side of Canada, but it's not got a drop of whiskey in it. That makes it suspect." Finch took out his flask and knocked back a shot, made a face then took a second drink.

"You're the Brit who threw the party, ain't you?" asked the big logger. "You look to be in worse shape than we are, but it was one hell of a blowout. The best ever!"

"I thank you kindly," Finch said. "Help yourselves to the water, though you must work the pump vigorously. I don't seem to be up to doling out even that small parcel of hospitality this morning."

Finch sat on the steps, watching the lumberjacks get their water. They pumped hard and got a trough filled for their horses.

"Much obliged," the logger said.

"You gave that poor steed too much water," Finch said suddenly. "The beast will bloat!"

"What's that? I never gave it that much," protested the logger.

"You did, sir. That creature can barely hobble along now."

"You call that hobbling?" asked the logger. "This is the fastest horse in Idaho, bar none."

"Come, come," Finch said dismissingly. "It has imbibed so much water it can hardly walk. And even if it were not so encumbered, it has the look of a decidedly torpid equine."

"Are you insultin' my horse?" The burly lumberjack trudged toward Finch, fists balled and looking like giant hams.

"Wait a minute," Slocum said, wondering if Finch was still drunk. He had to be, to pick a fight with a man capable of ripping him apart with no effort.

"No, no, Mr. Slocum, I know what I'm saying," Finch said. For a moment, his bleary eyes sharpened and Slocum almost believed him.

"You take that back, what you said 'bout my horse."

"Rather than mince words, why don't you prove it to me that your steed is capable and not as I have alleged."

"What?"

"I'm challenging you to a race. My horse against yours." Finch stood up, took a step and fell flat on his face. The lumberjacks laughed.

"He's in no condition," Slocum said.

"Am, too," Finch said, pushing himself up out of the dirt.

"What say we make this interesting?" the lumberjack said.

"You're not suggesting we bet, are you?" Finch sat cross-legged in the dust. "What stakes would satisfy your honor?"

"Ten dollars?"

"Pah! I didn't think you were serious," Finch said.

"Why, you—"

Slocum stepped between the logger and Finch. He was getting curious to see how this would play out.

"What do you consider a real bet, Finch?" Slocum asked.

"Fifty dollars," Finch said, slurring his words slightly. "And the winner gets the other's horse!"

"Done!" shouted the lumberjack. "Get your nag and we'll race."

"From where the fence has fallen down at the edge of the yard," Finch said, "around the tall pine tree yonder and back. The first one across the line wins."

"Let's race," the logger said.

"I need to get saddled." Finch hiccuped, then leaned heavily on Slocum. "Would you help me saddle my mount, Mr. Slocum?"

"He ain't takin' your place. You have to be the one doin' the racin'."

"Decidedly so, sir, yes, of course," Finch said. To Slocum he said, "Go saddle my horse and bring it here. I feel a little ... unwell." Finch turned and made weak retching sounds.

Slocum hurried to the barn, wondering about Finch. Was the Britisher putting on an act or was he so drunk he had no idea what he was doing? Either way, Slocum knew he would find out soon enough. And it wasn't likely to be pretty if Finch lost the race. The party the night before had cleaned him out to his last dime. Slocum doubted the lumberjack would much appreciate having to wait a month to collect his money and might take it out of Finch's hide.

Slocum didn't think he would do anything to stop him, either. Finch had to be taught responsibility some way.

"Yes, good, help me mount, will you, Mr. Slocum?"

Slocum cupped his hands, let Finch put his knee in them and let Slocum boost him up. Slocum stepped back and wondered again how drunk Finch was. The man had floated through the air and lightly dropped into the saddle.

"You want to bet more, limey?" asked another logger. "I got twenty dollars."

"I got another twenty."

"I have ten."

"Pikers, I'm puttin' up a hunnerd!"

Slocum took the loggers' money and held it. By the time they had finished upping the ante after seeing how drunk Finch appeared, he had almost two hundred dollars.

"See us to the line and ensure a fair start, will you, Mr. Slocum?" Finch wobbled and almost fell off his horse. The lumberjacks laughed in glee.

One sidled up to Slocum and asked in a loud voice, "That British guy, is he good for the bet? I don't want to win and then find he's flat-ass dead broke."

"He owns this spread," Slocum said. "That ought to be worth something."

"This place? It ain't worth the dynamite it'd take to

blow it up," the logger said. Then in a cagier tone, added, "Think he'd put it up for the bet? I was a wrangler down in Colorado for a spell. This place ain't the best for raisin' beeves, but it might be turned into somethin' else, with a lot of work. There's plenty of tall timber waitin' to be felled on this spread."

"I can't speak for him," Slocum said, "but I don't think Mr. Finch would argue much if you asked for the Rolling J instead of greenbacks."

"A whole damned ranch for two hunnerd dollars," muttered the logger. "We got that much 'n' more in timber on the land up near the mountain."

"Perhaps you'd care to increase your bet?" Finch asked.

"That's all we got," the mounted lumberjack said.

"Until next payday," Finch said shrewdly. Again Slocum couldn't tell if Finch was drunk or out to fleece the men.

"Double the bet," the mounted logger said. "I can beat him with my eyes shut."

"How's that, my good man? You want me to ride blindfolded?" asked Finch. "Very well. That'll keep me from seeing double."

They laughed when he pulled out a dirty linen handkerchief and fastened it around his eyes. Being blindfolded made Finch wobble even more in the saddle.

"Kin he still see?" asked one lumberjack suspiciously.

"What's the difference? Let's race!" cried the logger, his huge horse already tugging at the reins and ready to run.

Slocum led Finch's horse to the starting point, then asked in a low voice, "You know what you're doing, Finch?"

"Know? I don't have any idea, but win or lose it strikes me as jolly good fun!"

"Ready, set, go!" shouted Slocum. He jumped back as

Finch's horse shot off like a rocket. Slocum wasn't sure if it surprised him that Finch wasn't thrown from the saddle. If anything, the man showed perfect form, hunched forward, keeping low and using the reins to guide the horse as little as possible.

It was neck and neck getting to the tall pine, but Finch's horse cut inside the other, bigger horse and gained several strides on it coming back toward the finish line. The loggers cheered on their friend and then the cheers died as they saw how far Finch was outstripping him.

Finch flashed across the line, whipped off his blindfold and tossed it high into the air.

"Did I win?" he asked disingenuously.

"By about a hundred yards," Slocum said. In a lower voice, he said, "You really fleeced them."

"How dare you say that, sir? Wasn't the race fair?"

"I reckon it was, but I don't think they're going to be very happy."

"Nonsense," Finch said. "They will be quite happy with me. Wait and see."

The logger rode up, glowering down at Finch.

"You won," he said. "But you cheated. You weren't drunk!"

"Was I supposed to be even drunker than I already am?" asked Finch. He staggered a little and used his horse to hold him upright. "Double or nothing?"

"No," the lumberjack said, having learned his lesson. "That nag of yours is 'bout the fastest piece of horseflesh I ever laid eyes on."

"And yours is a fine stallion."

"Here's the money," Slocum said, passing over the loggers' bet to Finch. The Britisher stared at it, then looked up at the lumberjacks.

"I can't take your money like this," he said suddenly.

"What's that? You're giving it back?"

"I never said that. I'll buy any two other horses from

you for all the money," Finch said. He stepped back and let the loggers argue over which two of them would lose their horses or if they would let him keep their money.

Finch ended up with the burly logger's stallion and two mares.

The six men rode out, two to a horse, but with their money stuffed back in their pockets.

"See, Mr. Slocum? You need to have faith. They are happy that they did not lose a single farthing of their money, and I have three sturdy horses I didn't have when I woke up this morning with this beastly headache."

Finch turned and lost any food that might have been in his belly.

Slocum shook his head. He didn't understand Finch one little bit, but the man had talents he had not revealed before. The three fine horses standing near the ramshackle ranch house proved that.

7

"There," Slocum said, dusting off his hands. "The corral ought to hold your remuda, unless they get too rambunctious."

"Remuda? Ah, the horses, yes, I have heard that decidedly Spanish term before," Finch said, sitting on the top rail of the corral Slocum had rebuilt. He swung his feet as he looked at the three horses. "I think they are fine stock. They have the look of sturdy, dependable horses about them and would bring a fair number of equally capable foals into the world."

"Where'd you learn to ride like that?" Slocum saw that Finch was nowhere near as drunk now as he had pretended to be before and during the race with the lumberjack.

"All my family ride to the hounds. You know, after the fox? We would go out on a Sunday morning and chase about all day long. I grew to like it." Finch heaved a gusty sigh. "I miss the woods of yew and willow on the family estate, if not the hunting. It was quite brutal what the dogs did to the fox, you know."

"You weren't out to shoot it?" Slocum looked at the man, wondering if he had misunderstood him.

"Whatever for? That is the dogs' duty, not the riders'."
Finch made it sound as if it were somehow disagreeable
to shoot an animal for its meat or pelt.

"You can fix up your house without too much trouble.
The wolf left," Slocum said. "And the barn's in good
condition."

"I'm sure," Finch said dryly, as if it were a matter of
total unconcern for him.

Slocum climbed to the rail and gingerly sat a few feet
from Finch. The wood was old and seasoned and took
both their weights. For a moment, Slocum had worried
that it might have rotted through, like many of the corral
rails he had found.

"What else can you tell me about Randall Claymore?"

"That scoundrel!" cried Finch, suddenly animated. "He
tried to rob me! Me! The scion of an English lord!" His
ire subsided a little and he added, "Of course, I am the
second son, and that changes everything, doesn't it?"

"It doesn't change the fact he tried to rob you," Slocum
said.

"Do you think to win a reward if you bring him in?"
asked Finch. "I don't know of any bounty on his head.
The whole time I've been in Woodchip, I'd never heard
of him trying to rob anyone, although there have been a
number of loggers robbed upon leaving the Fancy Lady."

"Seems a bad time to rob anyone," Slocum said.
"They'd have spent their money on booze."

"Perhaps that condition of inebriation makes Claymore
think he has found easy prey. There is always the chance
that a man so besotted might also have been a big winner
in a poker game."

Drunks didn't end up winners too often at games re-
quiring skill. Slocum shrugged it off. Vultures like Randall Claymore didn't use good sense in their crimes.
Robbing a stagecoach or a bank made more sense than
trying to pick the pennies out of a drunk's pocket. The

risk was less in the latter crime, but so was the reward. Slocum knew that if he wanted to make a big score, he would look at robbing the logging company payroll.

In his day, he had been inclined to think of such things, but right now he had a legal, if somewhat onerous, chore to finish. He had to get Claymore to sign the papers. Then he could see about bringing a bit of justice to Idaho by turning Claymore over to the sheriff.

"You said Claymore hung out around Whiskey Lake. I looked over the lake and didn't see hide nor hair of him. Can you be more specific about where Claymore might be?" asked Slocum.

"I've heard Claymore works a gold mine near the lake."

"That's a strange place. I don't remember hearing of too many gold mines along a lakeshore," Slocum said. "Could he have a mine up in the hills around Whiskey Lake?"

"That is possible," Finch said, pursing his lips. "What do you say if I accompanied you to hunt for the scalawag? I don't know your business with him, but I intend to bring him to the bar of justice!"

"I don't have any trouble with that," Slocum said. "All I need is a few minutes of his time, then you can do whatever you like." Slocum hid his amusement at the notion that Finch could bring in anyone, much less a man who made his living as a petty thief. From everything he had heard about Claymore, he did not work any mine. That would be too hard a way to make a living for someone who preferred Spanish monte and a quick con followed by a hasty retreat.

"Bully," said Finch, hopping down. "Let me get my horse, and we can sally forth and find the beggar!"

Slocum got his Appaloosa saddled and led it from the barn about the time Finch trotted up. Watching the man on horseback amazed Slocum anew. Finch looked as if he had been born in the saddle and was part of the horse as it moved. For all his lack of skill when it came to repair work, Finch certainly rode well.

"To Whiskey Lake!" the Britisher cried, putting his spurs to the horse and rocketing away. Slocum followed at a more leisurely pace, seeing no reason to tire his horse needlessly. If they found Claymore, he might have to chase him down and wanted a fresh horse under him.

"This is pretty country," Slocum said. "How much of it is Rolling J land?"

"I cannot say, exactly," Finch admitted. "But it is forested and rocky. Where are the pastures for grazing the cattle?"

"The loggers think there are a few on the other side of the spread," Slocum said. He saw how the fences had been knocked over and never repaired. But at one time there had been fences. That meant someone had tried to run the ranch and had failed.

"Up this trail," Finch said, "and over the ridge so we can see most of Whiskey Lake."

They rode along the crest of the ridge, Slocum studying the blue lake and the land around it for any sign of men. After twenty minutes, he had to comment on the lack of activity.

"There's some old Indian superstition about the lake," Finch told him. "That might keep away those who are overly prone to worry about black cats and breaking mirrors."

Slocum doubted that. "Gold is a more powerful lure than any threat of an Indian ghost or curse," he said.

"That is so," Finch allowed. "But I seldom see anyone here when I come over."

"Why do you ride this way?"

"For the scenic beauty and the peaceful vistas, of course," Finch said, as if this explained everything.

"You sound more like a tourist than a rancher."

"I suppose so. This wilderness holds me unlike any country I ever saw in England. Perhaps it is good that I came to America," Finch said, but there was a wistfulness in his voice that Slocum took to mean Finch was lying to himself and that he missed his homeland.

"Let's ride down to the lake and have a look there," Slocum suggested. They made their way down the forested slopes and out onto a sandy beach that quickly turned to gravel. Slocum slowed and looked out across the lake to the few islands in the middle as well as along the shoreline for any trace of Claymore, mining or humans. Here and there he thought he saw hoofprints in the sand, but he could have been mistaken since the waves gently lapped up and masked any imprint.

"Have you ever seen anyone around the lake?" Slocum asked.

"Why, yes, of course, but not many, or often. Sometimes, at twilight, there are wagons that come and go. I always suspected they were supplying the miners."

"Do you see any mines?" Slocum looked around and saw nothing to show mining went on. For all the talk about gold, he didn't see any tailings, any rockers or other mining equipment. Still, he had heard from more than one source that Randall Claymore had come here to work a gold mine.

Slocum jumped to the ground and ran his fingers through the sand and gravel near the water at the side of a stream pouring into Whiskey Lake. He let it sift through his fingers so it caught the sunlight.

"What are you looking for?" asked Finch. "Gold?"

"Yeah," Slocum said, repeating the filtering a few more times. "All I see is what I'd expect from sand. Not even a glint of fool's gold. No quartz, nothing." He looked upslope at a stream meandering down from the heights, tumbling over rocks as it came. This was the spot where he would expect the heavy flakes of gold to deposit.

If there was any gold at all.

Slocum stood, brushed off his hands and then took a deep whiff of the air. He stepped away from his horse and sniffed at the air, trying to identify the odor.

"What is it? Has some unfortunate animal died?" Finch asked facetiously. "It's too much to hope that it is that scoundrel Claymore."

"I don't know what it is," Slocum said. "I thought something was burning."

"A forest fire?"

"This isn't wood, either dried or green. Not entirely." He sniffed a few more times but the scent had vanished. Slocum wasn't able to figure out what direction it had come from, either. "I don't reckon it matters, but it wasn't like anything I've smelled before."

"Is it worth pursuing?" asked Finch. From the way he spoke, Slocum knew the Britisher was tiring of the hunt for Randall Claymore.

"I can't say. I doubt it. Let's ride on a while longer before going back to your ranch."

"Ah, yes, my ranch," Finch said with some bitterness. "My worthless ranch that sucked up most of my money."

They rode is silence, Slocum's every sense alert. He saw a few rabbits and a deer coming to the water's edge to drink, but other than this wildlife, nothing stirred and the scent he had picked up did not return. He finally gave up riding along the deserted shoreline and signaled to Finch for them to head up the slope to the ridge and back to the ranch house.

Finch was unusually quiet on the way back. Slocum figured this was due to a variety of things. They hadn't found Claymore so the Brit could even the score, he dwelt on how he had been suckered and from the times his fingers drummed on his coat just over the pocket where he carried his flask, he was probably out of whiskey.

Slocum was happy enough to be left alone with his

own thoughts. He wanted to locate Randall Claymore as quickly as possible so he could return the papers to the Wichita lawyer and then return to Woodchip. Spending the winter with Maude curled up alongside him in bed seemed like a pleasant way to ride out a blizzard or two.

"You need to work on the fences if you're going to run any cattle," Slocum said. His statement jolted Finch out of his reverie.

"Ah, cattle. Yes, I suppose. Perhaps you would be so kind as to give me a few pointers, Mr. Slocum?"

"Let's ride over to the pasture just above your barn. I saw a few head of beeves there the other day," Slocum said. "You might be better off than you think."

It didn't take Slocum more than a few minutes after he spotted the ten scrawny cattle to realize Finch had gotten rooked.

"You won't be breeding those beeves," Slocum declared.

"I say, they are scrawny." Finch sniffed delicately, as if even discussing the condition of the cattle was distasteful.

"Go on, get a closer look at them and tell me what you see."

"Those poxy things?"

"They aren't diseased, just starved. They need to be moved to a pasture where there's more grass. But look them over and tell me what you see."

Finch walked around the cattle, venturing to touch one or two of them before returning and shaking his head in defeat.

"I don't see what you obviously have. Tell me, Mr. Slocum. What was I supposed to notice?"

"That's your breeding stock, right?"

"Why, yes."

"They're all steers." Slocum would have laughed except for the look of incomprehension on Finch's face.

"They're like gelding horses. Do you understand?"

"They're males without their, uh, equipment. Geldings. Yes, I see."

"You've been taken good and proper, if the rest are like these. You can't breed them."

"What would it take to put a herd on this ranch?" asked Finch.

"More than you're likely to make grazing them," said Slocum. "The grass is too sparse for many head. You might raise enough to supply Woodchip, but that's a close call."

"Hardly what I would call a windfall, eh?"

"You won't get rich at it," Slocum agreed. Something gnawed at the corner of his mind, but he found himself too distracted to rope and hogtie it at the moment. "Is there anyone around here already raising cattle? You might get a few strays off their herd, but you'd also be up against an established rancher."

"I know of a few head that come through, driven up from somewhere far to the south."

"So they bring in their beeves." Slocum thought this drove the final nail in the coffin for Finch. If it was more profitable driving cattle from the south, possibly Colorado or even farther down in Oklahoma or Texas, that meant no one was able to make a dime ranching.

They rode in silence as Slocum counted the head of cattle eking out an existence on the grass. They reached a larger pasture, one stretching over acres, but it was hardly enough to support a hundred head. Slocum had pegged that as a minimum amount for Finch to make a go of any ranching.

"This looks like splendid meadowland," Finch said.

"It is, and the fences keep the cattle out," Slocum said. "That's exactly the wrong way to graze an animal. You might want to round up the beeves and drive them over here."

"How many are there?"

"No more than twenty," Slocum said. Somehow, it didn't surprise him that Finch had no idea how many head he had bought. The man might have been drunk when he bought the Rolling J or he might have done it on a whim. "There might be more, but odds are against it."

Slocum swung his leg over the saddlebow and leaned forward slightly, stretching his back and feeling only a trace of discomfort from his wound.

"Why did you buy this place?"

"It struck me as a jolly good investment," Finch said haughtily. Then he slumped a little. "I wanted to show my family that I was capable of making my mark in the colonies."

"The colonies? Oh, you mean America."

"Yes, of course, that's what I meant. To be the second son and never to inherit is terrible. This is supposed to be the land of opportunity and I decided to seize it when I was offered an entire working cattle ranch."

It was pretty much as Slocum had thought. Finch wanted to impress his father with how well he had done and maybe make him feel a little guilty that he had turned out the son who was most capable. Instead, Finch was showing his family that he was a lost cause.

"You won't succeed with these beeves—these steers," Slocum said.

"From your tone you think there is another way?" Finch asked eagerly.

"It was something the lumberjacks said. The forests are your enemy right now, keeping grass from growing. Why not let them log a few acres and pay you for it? Then grass could grow and you'd have more pasture land in a year or two."

"No."

"What?" Slocum blinked at Finch's complete and total denial. "You don't have to cut the trees to increase your pasture lands. The loggers will *pay* you for the timber. You get money to live on and—"

"No."

Slocum knew better than to argue the point, although he wasn't sure why the idea so repelled Finch.

If anything, Finch was insulted by the notion of felling the trees and selling the lumber. Slocum shook his head, tugged at his Appaloosa's reins and headed back toward the ranch house. He had done what he could. Anything more that Finch wanted to do with the spread was up to him.

Somehow, Slocum doubted anything would be done.

8

The pounding of hammers driving nails greeted Slocum as he rode into Woodchip. He took a deep whiff of the air and caught the heady scent of freshly sawed lumber. As he rounded the bend in the road, he saw a half-finished building at the edge of town opposite the Fancy Lady Saloon. From the number of men working on it, the two-story structure would be completed in a day or two. Slocum was past being astounded at how fast such buildings went up in boomtowns, although it was hard to think of Woodchip as a boomtown.

There was no denying this was going to be a large building.

He rode past and headed for the sheriff's office at the far end of town. Slocum hesitated, then dismounted and went to the town jail. Although he had no reason to fear that Sheriff Pennant would have a wanted poster on him, Slocum felt he was tempting fate by bearding the lion in his den.

Pennant looked up from a newspaper spread in front of him on the desk and glowered.

"Whatya want, Slocum?"

"Information, if you have it, Sheriff," Slocum said. He

did not wait to be invited to sit in the single chair in front of the desk. Glued to the wall just behind the sheriff were several dozen faded wanted posters. Slocum didn't want to appear too concerned that one might carry his likeness. His eyes drilled into the sheriff's brown ones. Slocum couldn't help comparing their look with that of Maude's eyes. Hers were dancing and alive with merriment and promise. Slocum thought he stared into an open grave when he looked at Pennant's.

"I ain't no newspaper."

"That from Coeur d'Alene?" Slocum asked. "I don't remember seeing a newspaper office in Woodchip."

"Oro Fino," the sheriff said gruffly. "But you didn't come here to jaw about the news. Spit it out, then beat it."

"What do you know about Randall Claymore? I've heard tell he's prowling around these parts."

"Never heard of him," Pennant said. His eyes flickered for a moment, making Slocum wonder what he was hiding. "Now get out of my office."

"Thanks for the hospitality," Slocum said sarcastically. He stopped at the door and looked back. Pennant fixed him with his cold gaze, making Slocum think more of metal daggers than a grave now. "Aren't you interested why I'm looking for him?"

"That's your business, not mine."

"He tried to rob Finch the other night. That makes finding him your business," Slocum said, fishing to see how Pennant would respond.

The sheriff grunted and turned the page, pointedly ignoring Slocum.

Slocum stepped outside into the wan Idaho sun and looked up and down Woodchip's main street. There seemed more business being conducted than usual. He thought it had something to do with the building at the far end of town. On a whim, Slocum walked the length of town and watched the carpenters as they hammered and sawed and put up the walls on the second floor of the building. He finally walked over to the man who looked to be the lead carpenter.

"Howdy," Slocum greeted. "You're doing a fine job of erecting this building. How soon do you think it'll be open for business?"

"Thanks," the carpenter said, wiping dirty hands on his shirt. "I get a bonus if there's whiskey flowing by the end of the week. I don't see any reason this crew can't get it done a day or two early."

"Whiskey?" Slocum tried not to sound too interested.

"This is going to be the biggest dance hall in Idaho, bar none," the man said proudly. "I'm glad to have had a hand working on it."

"I didn't think the sheriff cottoned much to places selling liquor."

The carpenter shrugged. "Don't know about that. Me and my boys are from over in Coeur d'Alene. There's a legal paper nailed to that stud that's supposed to cover all the licenses."

Slocum walked to the post and quickly read down the page. Sheriff Pennant had authorized the sale of whiskey and beer, and this was the official permit. Slocum wondered how much it had cost in way of bribe to get the sheriff to allow another gin mill to be built. He read the permit again but didn't see what he wanted.

"Who owns this place?" Slocum asked. "I didn't see the owner's name on that permit."

The carpenter shook his head. "Don't rightly know who'll be running the place. All I know is that I was hired by a fellow in Coeur d'Alene and that he said he had taken care of everything. Me and the boys got here, found the lumber and nails and set to work."

"Who might that be that hired you?" asked Slocum.

"Never saw him before, but he went by the name of

Claymore. I was a mite worried about taking a job here until he put the full amount we're to get into the bank. It went into a special account. Can't remember the name of it but when we finish, we get the money that's already there."

"Escrow," Slocum said distantly.

"Yeah, that's what he called it."

"Thanks," Slocum said, heading back toward the other side of town and the Fancy Lady Saloon. He wanted to have a few words with Maude. Slocum smiled when he decided he might even ask about the new dance hall.

Slocum entered and saw Maude sitting at a back table, money spread out in front of her. She worked diligently to tally the receipts and never looked up until he sat down across from her. Maude jumped, then relaxed when she saw who joined her.

"You'll be my death, sneaking up on me like that, John."

"Didn't sneak," he said. "This is a lot of money to be flashing. Are you sure you want to count it here?"

"Nobody's coming in right now," she said, scowling. "The sheriff's special license only lasted till dawn of the day following Finch's party. Pennant checks now and again to be sure I'm not illegally selling booze."

"So where'd the money come from?" Slocum asked.

"It's my business reserve," Maude told him. "The sheriff's decided to let people buy licenses to sell liquor. If I want to compete with the new gin mill—"

"I saw it," Slocum interrupted. "It's mighty big and is bound to be open before the end of the week."

"That's why I have to buy my license as fast as I can so the customers get used to coming back to the Fancy Lady. If the owner of the new saloon brings in soiled doves or sells cheaper whiskey, I might find myself out of business."

"Who owns the place?" asked Slocum.

Maude shook her head, moved close to three hundred dollars into a pile and looked up when she saw him watching her like a hawk.

"That's how much Pennant wants," she explained. "Three hundred dollars for a year of licensing. It's highway robbery but what choice do I have?"

"You could move somewhere else," Slocum said. "It's not as if you had a lot of money tied up in this building. And you don't have any stock to move."

"There's some," Maude said. "The glasses; and the mahogany bar is my pride and joy. Getting all that shipped out of the county beyond Pennant's grasp would cost danged near as much as paying off the son of a bitch."

"You can buy whiskey and sell it with this license?" asked Slocum.

Maude got a strange look on her face. He guessed what else Sheriff Pennant was doing.

"You have to buy from dealers Pennant has approved."

"You ought to be in business, John," she said. "What really irritates me is that Ethan is the sheriff's only supplier. I have no idea what kind of unholy deal those two worked."

Slocum rocked back in the chair and thought hard. Did Ethan call the shots or was it the sheriff? Or was there someone else playing the tune that kept both of those men dancing? Someone like Randall Claymore?

"You've got a good crowd," Slocum said, pressed into a corner of the saloon.

"The loggers are waiting for the other place to open," Maude said. "See?" She pointed to a couple of the lumberjacks who occasionally went to the door and looked out, down the street toward the new saloon. "When it opens, I'll lose them all."

"The whiskey's good," Slocum said. "You sell at a fair

price, and then they come in to talk to you. That ought to keep most of them in the Fancy Lady."

"You're a dear," Maude said, "but I know what attracts men. If the new saloon has cribs and whores to put in them, the Fancy Lady will look like a ghost town. I don't cotton to women selling their bodies. Dancing and drinking with the customers is one thing, but no whoring. Call it a flaw in my nature, but I won't ever do it, even if I go bankrupt. Which I just might."

"They's openin'!" cried a logger in the doorway. "Let's go!"

Slocum had seen buffalo stampedes that were more orderly. As Maude had predicted, the lumberjacks shoved and pushed and got themselves through the door and tumbled out into the street before running pell-mell for the other saloon.

"Where's the party?" came a familiar voice. Finch entered the saloon and looked around in wonder at how empty the place was.

"Everyone's gone to the other saloon," Maude said. "Why don't you check them out for us, Finch?"

"But my friends are here! A round for everyone, my good man," Finch said to Sid.

"What have you been up to?" Maude asked.

"I have been exploring my spread, as it were," Finch said. "I am looking for some ray of hope that I can turn a profit on it. Alas, I have found only twenty-three head of cattle that Mr. Slocum tells me are all steers."

Maude looked at Slocum and said in a low voice, "Glad that condition's not catching."

"What do you think you'll do, Finch?" asked Slocum.

"I have no idea, but I will not allow those scruffy loggers to cut timber on my property!"

"You could make a few dollars and clear land for pasture," Slocum said. "Let me buy you a drink."

"Two bits each," Sid said, taking Slocum's greenback

and dropping it into a box under the bar. He dropped a few coins onto the bar in change. Slocum pushed them back as a tip. Sid made them disappear as fast as he had the greenback.

"Why don't you gents mosey down to the other place and bring me a report?" Maude said. "There might be something I can do to get the lumberjacks back in here and drinking—something, that is, I'd be willing to do."

"Your beauty ought to enchant them all," Finch said gallantly. "I see no reason to partake of liquor in some upstart melodeon when I can monopolize your time here. In fact, Sid, go to the piano and make yourself comfortable while you play something jaunty. I would like to dance!"

Finch held out his arm and Maude took it. Sid sat at the piano, cracked his knuckles and began playing. Slocum watched as Finch and Maude danced. Finch was as light as a feather on his feet and whirled Maude around and around in spite of the numerous bad notes Sid hit. As a piano player, he was a pretty fair barkeep.

Slocum finished his whiskey and quietly left. He saw that Maude noticed his departure but Finch did not. The Britisher was already drunk enough to not care what went on around him. Slocum pulled his hat down to protect his face from an increasingly cold wind blowing from the direction of the other saloon.

The NAUGHTY LADY DANCE HALL read a crudely painted sign swinging in the wind. Slocum put his head down against the stiff breeze and pushed into the smoky saloon.

It looked as if every lumberjack in Idaho was bellied up against the bar, but very few were at the tables. And Slocum didn't see any women going around to cadge drinks and seduce the loggers into spending their money on more carnal pursuits.

"They're comin'," one lumberjack said to Slocum.

"The women's comin' any time now. Have a drink while you're waitin'."

"That's a buck," the barkeep snarled.

"That's mighty expensive," Slocum said. "It'd better be good whiskey."

"The best you're likely to taste in Woodchip," the bartender snapped.

Slocum passed over a bill and got a shot glass filled with whiskey indistinguishable from that served in the Fancy Lady. It was good, burned as it went down his throat and pooled warmly in his belly—but Maude's accomplished the same result at a quarter the cost. The liquor's price would be more reasonable if there had been women here.

"Where are the ladies?" Slocum asked the barkeep.

"Comin'," was all the answer he got.

Slocum sipped at his whiskey and heard the grumbling around him. If the Naughty Lady charged so much for its rotgut and there weren't scantily-clad women running around to beguile the lumberjacks, why pay more for the whiskey? Especially since Slocum guessed that the Naughty Lady Dance Hall got its liquor from Ethan, as Maude did.

The conversation around him slowly turned in that direction without Slocum's intervention. He nursed his drink and looked around. The carpenters had labored hard but the place had several more days of work to be finished. The rickety stairs that led up to the cribs—or where they would be soon—wouldn't hold a puppy dog, much less the burly lumberjacks. If any of them tried to go up, he would find himself sitting on the floor with the collapsed staircase all around.

Even the bar wobbled with so many leaning against it. The owner had rushed to open the saloon.

"Who owns this place?" Slocum asked the logger next to him.

"What's the difference?" the lumberjack answered. "He's cheatin' us something fierce. Lookee here." He held up a shot glass. In his huge hand, the glass almost vanished. "Teeny lil shots o' whiskey and ten times what Maude charges!"

Slocum didn't bother correcting the man's arithmetic. He was right in principle.

"A new place has to recoup some of its opening cost," Slocum said.

"You keep your trap shut," the barkeep said, glaring at Slocum.

"Why's that? All I wanted to know is who the owner might be. I'd like to thank him personally for having such a fine drinking establishment." Slocum couldn't keep the sarcasm out of his voice.

"Ain't your business," the barkeep snapped.

Slocum subsided. What the man said was true. He didn't owe Maude anything and what good would it be finding out who owned the Naughty Lady? It changed nothing.

"You ever hear tell of a man named Randall Claymore?" Slocum asked the barkeep.

"What if I did?"

"There might be a few dollars in it for you. Might be as much as twenty." Slocum slid his stash from his pocket and riffled through the bills, then tucked them back. All the while, he watched the barkeep's eyes. The man looked around, shifty-like, and then licked his lips.

"Don't know the fella. Wish I did. I kin use the money."

"Might still be yours if you learn where I can find him. I don't mean him any harm. It's a private matter. Once I settle it, we'll both ride our separate ways."

"Yeah, right," the barkeep said, obviously not believing Slocum. Then the man hurried up and down the bar trying to goad the lumberjacks into buying more of the overpriced whiskey. Without women to hold their attention, the loggers were inclined to wander. When one came back in saying there was a dance going on at the Fancy Lady, the saloon emptied fast.

Slocum finished his drink and set the glass down with a loud click.

"Much obliged," he said to the irate barkeep.

Out in the street, Slocum heard Sid's loud, enthusiastic, off-key piano playing. As he started to return to the Fancy Lady, Slocum heard angry voices coming from beside the other saloon. He turned the corner and saw Ethan plainly but the man with his back to Slocum was obviously the one in charge. His finger stabbed out repeatedly into the bootlegger's chest as he upbraided him. The words were muffled, but Slocum made out enough to know the man was upset that his customers had left the Naughty Lady to return to Maude's saloon.

Ethan sputtered, then pointed. He had seen Slocum out in the street, watching and listening.

Somehow, Slocum wasn't too surprised that the man rebuking Ethan was none other than the county sheriff. When William Pennant spotted him, he turned as if he had been burned and ran off down the alley, leaving a gaping Ethan behind.

Slocum touched the brim of his hat, smiled and went on his way, whistling in time with Sid's loud piano playing.

9

The crowd lasted until after midnight; then the lumber-jacks began leaving by twos and threes to return to their camps. Sid was exhausted from playing the piano, but Finch was delighted and drunk as a lord. Maude had let him tend bar while Sid was otherwise occupied. Slocum had watched Finch for a few minutes and thought the man drank a shot for every two he served.

If that were true, Finch was in remarkably good shape for someone who ought to be pickled to the gills. Slocum guessed that vice required practice, and that Finch practiced constantly.

"We made a young fortune tonight," Maude said, look-ing at the box overflowing with money. She laughed and added, "Even if Finch drank up half the profit!"

"I had a jolly good time, dear lady," Finch said. He took her hand and bent to kiss it. The Britisher lost his balance and both Slocum and Maude had to catch him before he fell to the floor. "Thank you. Those earthquakes are so unpredictable," he said.

Slocum looped his toe around a chair leg and pulled it over so Finch could sit. As the man began to go to sleep, Slocum pushed the chair to the table so Finch could put his head down on his arms. In a few minutes he was snoring loudly.

"He's quite a character," Maude said. Her soft brown eyes fixed on Slocum. "And you're quite a man. What do you say we go upstairs so you can remind me—all night long?"

"Hey, Maude, Ethan's out back and wants to talk to you," shouted Sid from the storeroom.

"Business, always business," grumbled Maude.

"I'll go with you," Slocum said, a feeling in his gut that wouldn't go away.

"What's wrong?" Maude instantly saw how he reacted.

Slocum forced himself to relax, but he took the leather thong off the hammer of his Colt Navy and started for the back room, which lead to the alley behind the Fancy Lady. Maude hurried along, her skirts swishing softly as she muttered under her breath.

"God Almighty, you're not Maude," Ethan said, backing away when he saw Slocum instead of Maude. When the woman came out the back door to join Slocum, Ethan sidled along the rear wall of the saloon and looked at her. "What's he doin' here?"

"Just visiting," Maude said. "What's on your mind?"

"I . . . I got to charge you more for the whiskey. Now that there's competition in town, I cain't furnish to you alone. You got to at least match what they's payin' me down the street."

"Why, you miserable little sneak-thief!" cried Maude, stepping forward. Slocum held her back.

"How much?" Slocum asked.

"A hunnerd dollars a barrel. And that's cheap! You cain't get it from Coeur d'Alene no more. I know all 'bout them road agents!"

"I'll bet you do," Slocum said.

"I'd have to sell the whiskey at two dollars a shot to break even!" Maude said, after figuring out her expenses.

"And the Naughty Lady's only selling for a dollar a shot," Slocum said. "Isn't that a coincidence?"

"I gotta make money!" whined Ethan. "I like you, Maude, and you always played fair with me, but things have changed. We can't do business like we was."

"The sheriff owns the Naughty Lady, doesn't he?" asked Slocum. This brought Maude around to stare at him intently. "You work for Pennant, too. That's what the argument was about outside the other saloon."

"The sheriff cuts off my supply of whiskey, opens a rival saloon then cons me out of a license fee! Why, that skunk!" raged Maude. "You wait right here, Ethan. I want to send Pennant a message." She ducked into the back room.

"What're you lookin' for?" Slocum heard Sid ask her.

"The bung starter and the corkscrew. I got some serious work to do out back," the brunette said.

Hearing Maude's words built a fire under Ethan. He dodged Slocum's grab for him, then sprinted down the alley toward the far end of town. Slocum lit out after him. He had questions he wanted to ask, and not all of them were about the sheriff's crooked schemes. Both Pennant and the barkeep in the Naughty Lady knew more about Randall Claymore than they were letting on. Slocum wanted to find out if Ethan did, too.

He rounded the last building in town and ran smack into Sheriff Pennant. Slocum bounced back, swung around to keep his balance and knew he'd be dead in a split second if he turned to face the lawman. The dull click of a double-barreled shotgun being cocked was unmistakable.

"You won't shoot a man in the back, Pennant," Slocum said. "That'd cause folks to ask questions you wouldn't want to answer."

"Turn and face me, Slocum."

"If I do that, you'll cut me down." Slocum stood with

his back to Pennant, sweat beading his forehead. He had gotten himself into a pickle and didn't see how he could get out. If he drew his six-shooter, spun and tried to fire, he would be playing into the crooked lawman's hand.

"You're damned right I'd gun you down," Pennant snarled. "You blow into town and are within an inch of ruining one sweet deal, the only one I was ever able to get to work out for me."

Slocum kept his hands outstretched—and empty.

"Looks like we got ourselves a Mexican standoff. I can't throw down on you without turning around and you're not going to shoot me in the back. There'd be too many upstanding citizens of Woodchip who would wonder why you killed a man who wasn't looking at you."

"You're running away after shootin' at me," Pennant said. "That's what I'll tell them. I—"

"John!" cried Maude, running up. Sid was right behind her. And dragging along a few yards after the barkeep came Finch, looking bleary-eyed but sober enough to know what was going on.

"You have too many witnesses now, Sheriff. Unless you want to start a wholesale killing." Slocum worried that Pennant might be backed into a corner and would fight like the trapped rat that he was. The only good luck he saw was that the sheriff had a double-barreled scatter-gun and would have to reload if he shot Slocum and Maude. Finch and Sid might escape and raise the alarm before Pennant could shove two more shells into their chambers.

"You folks back off now, hear?" shouted Pennant. "I'm arrestin' Slocum."

"He wants to kill me," Slocum said.

"What are you arresting him for, Sheriff?" asked Maude. She held a mallet used to drive spigots into beer barrels in one hand and a corkscrew in the other. She hadn't been joking when she had gone hunting for them.

"Disturbin' the peace, that's what." Pennant moved closer, intent on plucking Slocum's six-gun from its holster. Slocum stepped away and kept the lawman at a distance. It was risky, but he couldn't do anything else without getting a double load of buckshot in his spine.

"I've been asking after Randall Claymore and that's spooked the sheriff," Slocum said.

"Reckon there might be more to it than that. Isn't that so, Sheriff Pennant?" demanded Maude. "What kind of a deal have you worked with that no-account bootlegger Ethan Moore?"

"H-he runs the new saloon," Pennant said, obviously lying. "He paid me for all the licenses, so that's a legit operation."

"So's the Fancy Lady Saloon," said Maude. "I paid, too. And you promised me my employees were off-limits for minor offenses like disturbing the peace."

"What are you sayin'? Slocum isn't no employee of yours!"

"Why, my dear constable," spoke up Finch, "however can you make that claim? I am a regular customer at the Fancy Lady and see everything that goes on there."

Slocum watched Maude and Finch closely and saw they were playing off each other. Maude might be lying but Finch wasn't, not in the strictest sense. That still shook Pennant's confidence in being able to kill Slocum. Slocum kept his mouth shut, and so did Sid. The barkeep backed off and tried to press himself into the wall of the bakery to keep from getting ventilated, should the sheriff open up with his shotgun.

"That's only good on the premises of the saloon," Pennant said. "I caught Slocum makin' a ruckus away from the Fancy Lady."

"As a trusty employee, he was only doing my bidding, Sheriff. Why not arrest me, since I ordered him to go after Ethan? I wanted to place another order with *our* moonshiner, and he took off before I could tell him what I wanted." Maude bore down on the fact that both she and the sheriff got their liquor from the same bootlegger. She tapped the bung starter against the side of the corkscrew, further flustering Sheriff Pennant.

"I'll let him off this time, but you keep him on a short lease, or I swear it'll go damned hard next time." Pennant stalked off toward the Naughty Lady.

"He wanted to murder you, John," Maude said in an awestruck voice. "I can't believe it."

"Believe it," Slocum said. "Pennant's not an imaginative man."

"Calling his saloon the Naughty Lady when the other is the Fancy Lady, and aptly named after its delightful proprietress, too," chimed in Finch, "shows how little mentation occurs in that poor fool's cerebellum."

"Yeah, whatever he said," muttered Sid. "Can we get back to the saloon? I feel exposed out here."

"Go on home, Sid," Maude said. "And you look clear-headed enough to return to your spread, Finch."

"Ah, yes, I see how it is. A gracious good night to you. I would bid you sweet dreams but I doubt you will be doing much sleeping," said Finch. Laughing, he headed for the livery stable, his step sprightly, if a little off now and then.

"Drunk as a lord," Maude said. "But he handles it well."

"You won't be buying any more whiskey from Ethan," Slocum said, retracing his steps with Maude at his side. He knew Finch could return to the Rolling J without any help. His horse knew the way better than its rider. But other matters in Woodchip required their immediate attention, and a supply of whiskey was foremost in Slocum's mind.

"So what? I'll find a way to get the tarantula juice. I always have." Maude steered him into the back room, closed and barred the door, then went into the darkened saloon. Sid had already closed up the front doors.

"With the sheriff—" Slocum started. Maude put her finger against his lips to quiet him.

"You talk too much, John. Look around you. We're all alone in this big place and can do anything we want. Anything. Do you really want to waste the opportunity by talking about Pennant and Ethan?"

He kissed her. When she broke off the kiss, she laughed and said, "I knew you could find more fun things to do."

"I haven't even started yet," he said.

"Oh, now I'm getting interested. What did you have in mind?"

"We can play it by ear," Slocum said, dropping to his knees so he could run his hands under Maude's skirts. He felt around until he found her warm legs and then slowly worked up until his fingers were between her firm, strong thighs.

"Your ear's not what I want there," Maude told him, her breath coming faster now as he explored her nether regions. She gasped and shivered a little when he finally discovered that she wasn't wearing bloomers. "And your finger's not quite what I had in mind, either. But it'll do for the time being."

Slocum began unfastening the ties holding Maude's skirt with his teeth. She helped him a little but mostly leaned back, her elbows on the bar as he worked to get her naked from the waist down. Slocum looked up and thought he had found heaven. The impudent thrust of the woman's breasts formed a notch that framed her lovely face. And with his finger moving around in her most intimate recess, there was no hiding how excited she was.

"What now, John?" she said in a voice choked with emotion. Maude lifted one leg and draped it over his shoulder. Then she tensed her muscles and drew his face in to where he still fingered her. Slocum got the idea and applied his lips to her pinkly scalloped nether ones. This produced an even more pronounced moan of joy from Maude.

"So good, so nice, I'm so excited, John. Keep doing that. It's making me weak all over."

Slocum easily supported her as she began to sag from the emotions rampaging throughout her trim, compact body. As he tongued and licked and kissed, he let his hands move up her body until he found all the right ties and ribbons to free her from her corset. He looked up again and saw her breasts bouncing lightly, each capped by a visibly pulsing coral button.

Slocum began working his way up from between Maude's widespread legs. He kissed her belly, thrust his tongue into her navel then worked up to the deep valley between her breasts. He wanted to dally on each of the snowy slopes but felt the pressures mounting in his own body that threatened to drive him crazy if he didn't do something about them. Soon.

"Let me, John," Maude offered. She reached down and unbuckled his gun belt, then she pressed and squeezed and massaged the lump growing at his crotch until Slocum was close to passing out. When she finally freed him and let his thick manhood leap out, long and hard and ready, he almost lost control.

"Turnabout's fair play," Maude said, teasing. "Now you know what you've been doing to me."

He kissed her to keep from discussing the matter further. His hands roved over her trim body but hers homed in on his crotch and stayed there, stroking up and down his rigid length, toying with the hairy sac dangling beneath, giving him measure for measure what he had been giving her in way of arousal.

"You're mighty short," he said. "I tower over you."

"We can do something about that," Maude said, turning toward the bar. She put her hands flat on the slick mahogany bar, then climbed onto the brass foot rail. The provocative brunette shoved her snowy-white behind toward him, daring him to do something more.

Slocum saw that the extra height made everything about right. He put his hands on her hips and guided her to the exact spot he wanted. Then he entered her smoothly from behind.

Maude's feet slipped a little on the brass rail, but Slocum held her upright. He wasn't going to change a thing. He was buried in the clinging, tight, moist cavern and couldn't think of anywhere he wanted to be more.

"Oh, John, oh, oh!" she sobbed.

Maude lay flat on the bar, her breasts mashed so she could thrust her rump back into the circle of his groin. Then she began rotating her hips. Slocum began turning in the opposite direction. They stirred around like this until Slocum felt the heat boiling in his loins and knew he couldn't stand much more. He began thrusting in and out, moving faster and plunging deeper with every lunge forward. Maude began gasping and moaning incoherently. Slocum was in hardly better condition.

When he felt her clamp down firmly around his buried length, he could no longer withstand her charms. He spurted hard and fast as his hips took on a life of their own.

They strove together until Maude slumped down, then turned around to support herself with her elbows on the bar as she faced him.

Sweat sheened her face and body. Slocum watched in fascination as a drop of sweat ran down from Maude's throat into the deep valley between her naked breasts. Impulsively, he bent forward and captured it with a quick swipe of his tongue.

"You're incredible, John. I've usually tired out most men by now. But not you."

"What makes you think I'm not all tuckered out? That was pretty exhausting."

"I don't know," Maude said. "It must have been something you said. Or did. Or the way you looked at me." She jumped up and sat on the bar. The brunette leaned back and lifted her feet to the edge so she was wantonly exposed to him. "If there's anything on the menu you want, you'd better get it 'fore the store closes."

Slocum found himself stirring again. He moved forward and sampled what he could before Maude pulled him up onto the mahogany bar with her. The next thing he knew, the morning sun was slanting through the front windows and neither had gotten a wink of sleep.

Slocum wondered if Finch could predict the future or if it only had been a lucky guess on the Britisher's part. Or had it been so obvious even a drunk could see what Slocum and the sultry saloon owner were heading toward? Whichever it had been, Slocum gladly passed up a night's sleep for the time he and Maude had spent together.

10

"Some days I don't want to get up," Maude said, stretching so that she reached high above her head and caused her shapely breasts to flatten. Then she relaxed, and they popped back into shape.

"Better get dressed," Slocum advised, pulling on his pants. "You don't know when the first customer'll be by, wanting to wet his whistle."

"I'm glad I had a chance to wet your whistle, if that's what you want to call it," Maude said, grinning ear to ear.

"Were you serious about having another supplier for your whiskey?" asked Slocum, settling his gun belt around his waist. The time for play was past, and he had enough other things on his mind to keep him occupied all day long. "Ethan's not going to sell to you anymore, even if the sheriff lets him."

"I can order it from Coeur d'Alene, or maybe Oro Fino. It might take a dozen guards to get past the road agents, but I swear I'll do it before I give in to the like of Will Pennant!"

Slocum liked her fire, though he suspected Maude was biting off more than she could chew. She went up against Ethan and the sheriff, but there had to be more involved than that. For starters, he reckoned all the masked high-waymen who had destroyed much of Maude's last whiskey shipment were part of the gang.

"Where does Ethan get his liquor?" Slocum asked suddenly.

"Why, I—" Maude looked surprised. "I never asked him. It's right-good whiskey. Strong, smooth. Better than I could make on my own."

"The sheriff would never let you set up a still," Slocum said.

"I'll find someone who can get me cheap whiskey, John. Don't worry. I've been in this business for a spell and have seen about everything there is to see." She moved closer to him and ran her fingers over his arms, his chest, lower. "I wouldn't mind seeing some of it again, though."

Slocum kissed her and then pushed her away.

"I'll go find out if Finch made it back to his spread," Slocum said.

Maude laughed. "You feel like you have to watch out for him, too? He's like a little puppy dog, all eager and getting into trouble but you just can't find it in your heart to punish him when he makes a mess because it's so cute."

"I don't think Finch is cute," Slocum said curtly.

"Get on out of here, John. I need to clean up and then do inventory to see what's left in the kegs. We did a ripsnorter of a business last night, in spite of the Naughty Lady's grand opening."

Slocum left, taking care to look around for the sheriff when he got to the street. He reached over to his cross-draw holster and made sure his Colt was riding easy at his hip. Slocum knew how close he had come to being gunned down by the sheriff the night before. Given the chance, Pennant would shoot him from ambush and make it look as if someone else did it.

Slocum heaved a sigh of relief when he got out of Woodchip and onto the road leading to Finch's ranch. He felt better surrounded by trees and mountains and land that he loved. It was no secret that he didn't hanker much for other people's company, especially in towns. Too many people, not enough space.

He found the weed-overgrown road leading to Finch's ranch house and was surprised to find the man already out and about. Finch was leading a steer toward the barn.

"You planning on milking it?" Slocum joked.

"Ah, Mr. Slocum. No, I have figured out the full depth of the confidence game played on me. A steer will give nothing but a steak or two."

"You're learning," Slocum said, jumping down. "While I was riding out here, I did some thinking."

"About how to get rid of the steers, other than by eating them?"

"No," Slocum said. "That's all they're good for, and maybe not then." He ran his hand over the steer's flank, noting the way its ribs stuck out. There wasn't much meat on the bones.

"I need to render them for tallow, to make candles and such items," Finch said. From the way he spoke, Slocum knew the man had no idea what he was talking about.

"Meat," Slocum said firmly. "Sell the steers to the loggers. Their cooks would jump through hoops to get fresh meat cheap."

"I detect a germ of something more growing in your statement," Finch said. "What else are you suggesting that I do?"

"You rode like a champion the other day against the lumberjack," Slocum said. "You knew what to look for picking the best of their horses, too."

"Of course," Finch said. "I grew up riding to the hounds. I helped my father's trainer whenever I could."

Finch smiled wryly. "It got me out of the house and away from my loathsome older brother."

"You know about breeding horses?"

"And training," Finch said. "Are you suggesting I sell the steers and go about raising horses? My word!"

"You don't have enough pasturage for a big herd. But fifty head of horses would bring you enough money to keep the spread going."

"Are the extant meadows enough for grazing such a small herd?" asked Finch.

"You tell me," Slocum said. "Remember what you did growing up. What do you think?"

"By Jove, yes! It is more than enough. I might be able to graze twice that. For cattle it is not enough by ten, but for horses, yes!"

"Men need horses real bad out here," Slocum said, looking at his Appaloosa. The stallion whinnied. "They're willing to pay for good ones, especially ones already broken to the saddle."

"I can do this! Why, the prospect actually excites me. It seems like it would be fun!"

"How many head of cattle have you already rounded up?" asked Slocum. "I can drive them to the logging camp and see if I can't interest them in some steaks on the hoof."

"Three," Finch said. "That's all I've located this morning."

Slocum looked at the Britisher and marveled that he didn't act the least bit hungover after his binge the night before.

"That'll do for a start. Might be, I can get a contract for a few beeves a week until the entire herd is sold off."

"I want to thank you, Mr. Slocum. This is most considerate of you to help a poor bloke like me."

"You helped me last night when the sheriff was so intent on cutting me in half with his scattergun."

"Oh, that was nothing. The sheriff's bark is far worse than his bite."

Slocum didn't think so but was not going to argue with Finch over how dangerous Pennant might be. He found the other two steers Finch had corralled next to the horses, got the beeves moving with well-placed slaps on their scrawny rumps and then mounted.

"I'll be back by sundown," Slocum said.

"If you are too late, I may well be in Woodchip, celebrating my good fortune in finding a future for myself."

Slocum took his lariat from his saddle and ran out a few feet of hemp to use on the steers' hindquarters whenever they tried to veer from the path he chose. The closer they got to the logging camp, the more nervous they became, as if they understood what their fate might be.

"Howdy," Slocum called when he saw the cook wiping off a knife on his apron. "Am I in time for chuck?"

"You a new lumberjack?"

"No, can't say that I am. I've worked out on the coast, but I'm not hunting for a job with a saw today."

"Then I can't feed you," the cook said, not looking at Slocum. "Those are about the scrawniest cows I ever laid eyes on."

"They can be yours for a price," Slocum said, swinging into a sales pitch that ended up with him sharing a cup of coffee with the cook as they dickered over the price. Slocum got more than he had hoped for the three steers, plus the promise of selling three more the following week if none of the lumberjacks complained about the meat.

"I wondered why nobody ever came around tryin' to sell to us." The cook spat some of his coffee into the cooking fire. It flared, telling Slocum the cook put more than coffee into his cup.

"Nobody at all comes around? Not even gents like Randall Claymore?"

"Claymore? What's he sell? Beef on the hoof?"

"He hangs out around Whiskey Lake, so I thought you might know him," Slocum said.

"Nobody hangs out there," the cook said, shaking his head vigorously. "Too dangerous in that neck of the woods. Some of the boys went over to the lake lookin' for fun when we first started logging here. Well, two of them never came back."

"Road agents?"

"Might have been. We never even found their bodies. The other three with them hightailed it with some of the craziest stories you ever did hear. They were drunk, so they found some swill along the way, since nobody gets that soused on lake water."

"Where are these three? I'd like to talk to them. I've ridden along the shore of Whiskey Lake a couple times and never saw anything, much less bandits."

"Them? They're long gone. You got to know how loggers can be. These three got spooked at losing two friends and hightailed it when they sobered up. Took a couple weeks to find new lumberjacks. You sure you don't want a job? If you worked the big trees, like you said, chopping down these teeny little twigs ought to be a snap for you."

"Got a job," Slocum said, thinking about the lumberjacks who had gone to Whiskey Lake and run afoul of—what?

"Not sayin' we don't need the beef," the cook declared, "but I am sayin' we can use help fellin' trees a whole lot more."

"Where did those gents go when they ran into the road agents at the lake?" asked Slocum.

"Lemme see," the cook said, taking a big swig of his whiskey-laced coffee. "We been movin' to the north as we cut down the trees. That'd make the camp then 'bout there." He pointed. "Straight over the ridge from there and down to the lake's what they said."

"Much obliged," Slocum said.

"If you think you're in my debt, then pick out a few fatter cows next time."

Slocum laughed and bid the cook good-bye. He headed straight for the old camp. The road was broad and smooth where the heavy wagons had rolled out their load of timber. Even if there hadn't been such a good road, he would have had no trouble finding the old logging camp. The vegetation had been trampled flat for yards around a big firepit. The trash stacked up waist-high drew flies and carrion animals. Slocum drew his bandanna up to keep out some of the stench of unburied, rotting garbage as he got his bearings.

"Over the ridge," he muttered, finding the direction quickly. With some pleasure he left the abandoned camp and soon got away from the malodorous site. He came to the top of the ridge. Trees had been felled all around, giving a clear view of Whiskey Lake. It gleamed like silver as the sun reflected off its gently rippling surface.

Again, Slocum saw no human activity around the lake-front. This bothered him because so much fresh water was the obvious watering hole for huge herds of cattle. Men needed water and drilling for it or carrying it far in the mountains was hard work. Better to simply walk out the back door to the lake and grab a bucket.

No houses were visible anywhere he could see.

"But there is a well-travelled road," he said, the sun catching the land along the eastern shore just right so he could see the twin ruts cut in the sod. "Who uses that road? The loggers?"

Slocum looked around for sign that the lumberjacks felled their trees and then shipped them down along that road. If there had been water enough in any of the smaller creeks feeding into Whiskey Lake, Slocum would have thought the cutters would use the rivers to float their logs to the lake, push them to the end and then load them on wagons for shipment. Moving a big log in the water was faster and easier than having a team of mules drag it out.

When he reached the road, Slocum dismounted and knelt to examine the tracks. Heavy wagons rolled along this road and had passed by recently. But he couldn't figure out which way they ran.

"Both? Loaded as they travel in one direction and empty in the other?" But Slocum couldn't find any wagonwheel tracks that were lighter. Either the wagons went in one direction only or were loaded as they went in both directions.

Slocum shivered as an afternoon wind whipped across the lake, causing small whitecaps to buck and dodge on the watery surface. Birds circled above, keen eyes fixed on the surface for any sign of fish in the lake. Then they began disappearing as the wind built to a strong gale.

For the briefest instant, Slocum caught the odor he had scented a few days before. Then it was gone on the wind. But rather than track down the strange smell, he was more interested in sounds caught and carried on the stiff breeze.

". . . Pennant," came the fragment of a sentence.

Slocum mounted and stood in the stirrups to find the source of the conversation. Near a clump of pines stood three men, two with their backs to him. Squinting, Slocum made out the identity of the man facing in his direction.

Ethan Moore.

It didn't take much of a leap of faith to believe one of the other men was Sheriff William Pennant.

Slocum rode at an angle from the road, then dismounted and left his Appaloosa in a thicket so he could advance on foot. He wanted to spy on the sheriff and find out what brought him and his bootlegger out to Whiskey Lake.

"There's gonna be trouble, I tell you, Pennant," whined Ethan.

"There's always trouble, and I'm givin' you the same answer I always do. I'll take care of it."

"That woman's the real trouble. Burn her out," said the third man. Slocum tried to get a good look at the man's face but couldn't. The man had his Stetson pushed high on his forehead so the entire hat hid the back of his head, making it impossible to even tell the color of his hair.

"In Woodchip? A fire would destroy the whole damned town," declared Pennant. "No, she'll be out of business soon enough. She can't get enough whiskey, and what she'll be sold will be ten times too pricey."

"I kin do that, Pennant," Ethan said quickly.

"You fool," snapped the third man. "You haven't understood a word we've said. You don't sell to her no more. All the whiskey goes through the sheriff's saloon. And I make sure she doesn't freight in any supplies. When she's out of business, we'll have the whole danged town to ourselves."

"Why bother? Woodchip's not so big," Ethan said.

"It will be, it will be," the sheriff assured him. "Don't worry your head none. Let us do the thinkin' and plannin'. All you'll have to do is figure out how to spend all the money you'll get."

Slocum cocked his head to one side to catch the rest of what Pennant had to say. Something was going to happen to make Woodchip a real boomtown. Anyone owning the sole saloon then would stand to make more than a young fortune. But as he waited to hear what else the sheriff might say, the third man spoke.

"Get back to work, Ethan," he ordered. "And you, Sheriff, you get on back to town. I got work of my own to tend to."

If there had been any question who was the boss, this ended it. Both Ethan and Pennant took their orders from the third man. Slocum edged around, moving carefully through the brambles, to get a better view of the leader. He froze when he heard Pennant's comment.

"Don't go gettin' high and mighty on me. We're partners in this."

"All right, Sheriff, whatever you say." The man turned and Slocum finally got a good look at him, a ray of afternoon sun illuminating his face.

Randall Claymore.

11

Slocum watched as Sheriff Pennant rode off, following the lakefront in the direction of town. Ethan grumbled and argued with Randall Claymore a few minutes more and then stalked off on foot, leaving Claymore behind.

Slocum started forward, then saw he would never catch Claymore in time. The man went to the small stand of trees nearby, brought out a horse, mounted and rode off in the opposite direction the sheriff had taken. Slocum raced back to where he had left his Appaloosa, jumped into the saddle and lit out after Claymore. If he could catch the man before he vanished into the countryside, getting the papers signed would be a snap. After that, he would have to consider how best to deal with the man.

Claymore had, after all, tried to rob Finch. And whatever else he was mixed up in affected Maude. From what Slocum could tell by spying on the trio, there was a difference of opinion between Claymore and Pennant as to who was in charge. Wearing a sheriff's badge gave Pennant an advantage, but Slocum had the feeling Claymore was the real power behind their scheme.

Whatever it was.

He reached the twin ruts cut through the grass and

110

quickly picked up Claymore's hoofprints. Slocum looked ahead along the road, but it twisted back and forth as it followed the snakelike Whiskey Lake shore. Horse protesting, Slocum galloped after Claymore. Slocum wasn't sure what the best way to approach him would be. If Claymore recognized him as the man who had saved Finch, Slocum knew he might be in for a hard time. Or if Claymore had been skulking around Woodchip and had met with Pennant, even getting close to the man would be impossible.

Slocum now regretted having been so open in asking Pennant about Claymore.

Looking around, Slocum hunted for any trace of a gold mine. The hills rose sharply away from Whiskey Lake, but only trees stretched up the slopes. He didn't see any mine with its tailings sneaking downhill. If Claymore had a gold mine in this region, he kept it a secret.

For all that, Slocum saw no mines at all. From his brief exploration along the ridges above Whiskey Lake, the rock didn't have the right composition for either the carbonates that gave up silver or the quartz holding precious gold. The few streams meandering down the sides of the hills had not been too productive in bringing down flecks of gold from higher on the slopes, either.

This was logging country, not mining. Over at Coeur d'Alene there might be valuable mines, but not on the banks of Whiskey Lake.

"Where's the son of a bitch?" Slocum wondered aloud. He slowed his headlong pace and listened hard for the sound of Claymore's horse. The wind whipping over the lake and through the tall pines were the only sounds reaching his ears.

Slocum jumped to the ground, walked along slowly as he studied the dirt in the road and the crushed weeds and grass. A rider had come this way recently. It had to be Claymore since there weren't any other tracks.

Looking up from the ground, Slocum half turned and inhaled deeply. He almost gagged on the smell carried on the wind. It was stronger than the previous times he had scented it along the lakeshore. This time it made his eyes water and his nose run. He swiped at his nose as he wondered what caused the stench.

"Who are you and whatcha doin' here?"

Slocum spun, his hand going for his Colt Navy. He froze when he saw Ethan Moore a dozen yards off, at the edge of the forested area higher up the slope.

"I know you! You're Maude's gunfighter!"

"Wait," Slocum said. "I'm here on business."

"The sheriff tole me all about your business!" Ethan slapped leather and dragged out a heavy Remington. He was no gunman. He clumsily cocked the thumb-buster and lifted it in Slocum's direction.

Slocum went for his own six-shooter and got it out, cocked and aimed before Ethan could center on his target.

"I'm not here to shoot it out with you, Ethan. I need to talk to Claymore on business. I don't mean you—or him—any harm."

"You—you—you—" sputtered the man.

Slocum had not believed Ethan would fire. The man's finger might have accidentally pulled the trigger or he might have been a lousy shot. Whatever the case, the gun bucked in Ethan's hand and a heavy slug whirred past Slocum, close enough to make him duck but far enough away that there was no chance he would be harmed.

Weaving, Slocum got his balance back and started to return fire. By now, Ethan had vanished into the woods. Slocum lowered his six-gun, wondering if it was worth going after Ethan or if he should keep on Claymore's trail. Then a question came to him that sent him plunging into the woods after Ethan. How had Ethan reached this point so fast when he had been on foot? The lake curled and all it would take to get here without following the road would be a hard trek up over the ridge, but even then Ethan had covered the distance fast.

Too fast for Slocum's liking.

He whistled for his horse. The Appaloosa trotted over, looked askance at him for being shot at and silently begged him not to repeat it, then let Slocum mount.

Slocum rode directly for the spot in the woods where Ethan had vanished and found the secret to the bootlegger's speed. Fresh horse droppings showed he'd had a horse tethered out of Slocum's sight back where Pennant, Claymore and Ethan had palavered.

"Ethan!" The cry echoed through the woods, then disappeared totally as the wind smothered the name.

The wind could not hide the report of the Remington firing a second shot in Slocum's direction. The heavy slug tore through a branch several feet to the right. The Appaloosa tried to buck, but Slocum held the reins firmly.

"I want to talk, Ethan. Nothing more."

This time, when Ethan fired on him, Slocum was ready. His sharp eyes followed the track of the bullet back through leafy branches and low-growing bushes. He lifted his six-shooter and fired once. A loud shriek of pain rewarded him.

"You damn liar! You said you wasn't gonna do nuthin' but talk!"

"Drop the smoke wagon and come on out, Ethan," Slocum shouted. "I don't want to kill you, but I will if you make me."

Again the frightened bootlegger surprised him. Ethan began firing wildly.

"You ain't gonna pin it on me. I didn't tell no one. I got to kill you, Slocum. I got to or they'll think I told!"

Slocum wasn't interested in finding out what Ethan was talking about. He was more concerned about staying alive. He fired another shot into the thicket to convince

Ethan he meant business. This time only silence greeted him.

"Come on out, Ethan. Hands up. I know your gun's empty, but I want to be sure you don't have a hideout piece."

Silence. The wind died down and left an eerie blanket of silence over the forest. Then the breeze kicked up again, bringing with it a chill as it whipped off the lake. Slocum caught the nose-wrinkling smell once more but couldn't investigate its source.

He saw a foot sticking out from the bushes where Ethan had hidden.

Slocum rode through the forest, ducking low-growing limbs and making his way through to a point to one side of the bushes. He was a good shot but not so good that he could have drilled Ethan smack in the middle of the forehead from that distance. The man lay sprawled on his back, a startled expression on his face.

"You stupid son of a bitch," grumbled Slocum. He hadn't meant to kill Ethan. There were too many questions he wanted answers to for him to murder his only source.

Slocum rode closer and saw that Ethan had died instantly from the slug between the eyes. It was a shot in a million, but it had ended Ethan's miserable life.

As Slocum started to dismount, he heard sounds from farther upslope that caused him to settle back into the saddle.

A dark shape moved. And another and another. When Slocum saw three mounted men, he knew he had to get away. All had rifles aimed in his direction.

He ducked low as he turned his Appaloosa around to retreat to the lake when the first flight of singing bullets ripped past him. The closest slug tore splinters from a gum tree and spattered him with sticky sap. Riding hard now, he reached the road and looked in the direction Claymore had taken. He had to retreat in some direction. Should he go after Claymore?

Self-preservation told him not to. The riders reached the edge of the forest, stopped and began firing at him with deadly intent. If Slocum trailed behind Claymore, he might find himself caught between the trio of riders and Claymore. If he rode in the direction taken by the sheriff, the worst that could happen was Claymore joining the three behind him.

By now Sheriff Pennant was long gone and not a threat. But the riflemen definitely were. Every round they fired came a few inches closer. It wouldn't be long before they found their range and left Slocum's bullet-riddled body on the shore of Whiskey Lake.

His horse didn't need to be spurred to gallop like the wind. The powerful stallion put a considerable distance between them and the pursuing riders, but Slocum saw he was wrong about the sheriff. The lawman had not returned to Woodchip; now Slocum saw him in the distance, riding toward real trouble.

Almost at the spot where the sheriff had met Claymore and Ethan, Slocum sawed at the reins and turned his Appaloosa's head. He barreled upslope again, retracing the route he had taken getting to Whiskey Lake. Before he knew it, his lathered and out-of-breath horse had taken him to the logger's first camp.

Slocum looked around for something to turn to his advantage. All that had been left were piles of rotting garbage. Just breathing here was a chore. He might dismount, take his Winchester and shoot the riders as they came up the hill after him, but Slocum knew he could never hold off three men for long. If the sheriff joined them, there would be four against him.

And he had seen at least two others in the forest near where Ethan had been killed. They had been afoot, but Ethan had surprised him by having a horse nearby. The vaguely seen men on foot might also have their mounts close at hand. Fighting Ethan was one thing, taking on an entire gang of outlaws was something else.

Slocum knew he faced a veritable army. Even taking a potshot here and there wouldn't stop them if they were intent on avenging Ethan—or silencing someone who might have seen too much.

Slocum wished he knew what it was that he might have seen. That would help him figure out what to do now.

"Come on," he urged his exhausted horse. He got the stallion walking slowly, then picked up the pace, slowed to a walk and carefully returned to a trot. Varying the gait let the Appaloosa rest a mite while continuing to put distance between him and the sheriff's gang.

As he rode, Slocum turned over in his head everything that had happened. Was it Pennant's gang? Or Claymore's? That they were also the road agents who had tried to hijack Maude's whiskey shipment seemed an easy guess. They had a camp around Whiskey Lake, and from the way Ethan Moore had shot first and not wanted to talk at all, they were jealously guarding it.

Ahead, Slocum saw the new logging camp. He considered going to them for help, then decided against it. There was no reason to involve the lumberjacks in his trouble. They wouldn't be of much help, in any case. Most of them wore knives at their belts, the sharp blades being more useful than six-shooters.

Cutting through the woods, letting the sounds of the sawing and trees crashing to the ground fall behind, Slocum headed back for Finch's spread. The Rolling J might not give much in the way of shelter but it afforded Slocum a place where he could rest briefly and, if possible, negotiate with the men chasing him.

If the sheriff was with them, he didn't have a snowball's chance in hell. But if they were road agents, Slocum might talk his way out by claiming they had missed their real quarry. He didn't put much store in the results, but his horse was going to collapse under him if he pushed it hard for another few miles.

He topped the ridge and found the game trail he had used to get to the loggers' camp. It ran straight back to a meadow near Finch's barn. Slocum looked around for the Britisher but didn't see hide nor hair of him.

Slocum put his Appaloosa in the barn out of sight, then rested his Winchester against a fence post and hopped into the corral with Finch's three new horses.

"I say, old chap, you made it back!" cried Finch, stumbling from the house. If someone had tied yarn to him, he would have weaved a rug as he stumbled and staggered back and forth across the yard toward the corral.

"Get out of sight," Slocum called. "I've got road agents on my tail. They'll be here any time—"

A bullet whined past his head and embedded itself in the side of the barn.

"Seems as if 'any time' is now," Finch said, supporting himself by leaning heavily against the gate to the corral.

Slocum grabbed his rifle. He had hoped to put on a little act for the road agents to confuse them. They had trailed him long enough and had gotten a good enough look at him as they rode to not be so easily duped. Slocum rested the rifle on the top rail, sighted and squeezed off a shot.

He was expert with a rifle and winged the lead rider. Slocum wished luck had been on his side as it had when he had shot blindly at Ethan. He bore Ethan no malice, but he had ended up dead. The bandit he shot at now had already emptied a six-gun at Slocum and would see him in his grave.

"Missed," Slocum grated as he levered in another round. He had hoped to take the highwayman out of the fight entirely. "You see Sheriff Pennant with them?"

"The good high sheriff?" Finch climbed up to the top

rail, used his hand to shield his eyes against the setting sun and then fell off, landing heavily on the ground. He stared up at the sky, as if wondering where the country-side had gone. "I didn't see him. I don't see much but a few clouds and the sky. It's so blue, you know."

"They're not going to charge in now. They'll sit back a ways and take their best shots at us." As Slocum spoke, a slug ripped through the crown of his hat, sending it flying. He ducked, dived under the bottom rail of the cor-ral and fetched his hat.

"Won't be carrying much water in that anymore, old chap," Finch said, giggling.

"Water's not all I worry about leaking out of my hat," Slocum said. "If they get a decent shot at me, it'll be my brains pouring out."

"That's funny, Mr. Slocum. You are quite the jester, aren't you?"

Finch continued to lay flat on his back while bullets sang above. He was oblivious to the fight going on around him.

"We can't stay here, Finch. We have to hightail it back to town." Slocum wasn't sure that was a good idea, but it was better than staying here and waiting for the road agents to get reinforcements. Then an idea dawned on him. "Finch, can you ride in your condition?"

"My condition? Sir, of course I can ride in my con-dition. I am a true horseman, a veritable centaur. I—"

"Get on a horse and go tell Maude that Ethan's dead and that the sheriff might be coming around looking for me."

"I say, that seems a bit much to remember."

"Move!" Slocum shouted. He grabbed his rifle and went to the corner of the barn to head off a rider trying to circle and come at them from the side. He fired steadily and drove the man back.

Slocum looked over his shoulder and saw Finch precariously balanced on the upper rail. With a yelp, Finch jumped and landed astride the stallion. Slocum worried Finch couldn't ride bareback and then saw this wasn't a problem. The Britisher rode as if he had been glued onto the horse's back.

"Yeee-haaa!" Finch shouted as he jumped his stallion over the low corral fence and raced down the road toward Woodchip.

Slocum lay flat on the ground, silently waiting for the road agents to respond. It took them a few seconds to realize one of their quarry was getting away. Or maybe they thought it was Slocum. Whatever their reasoning, the trio rode directly for the barn —and Slocum's rifle.

He fired methodically. One man fell from his saddle. The second doubled over and fought to keep in the saddle. The third man caught at least two slugs, both in his left arm. Slocum fired until his magazine came up empty, giving the outlaws the chance to help their fallen comrade back into the saddle.

They retreated, the worse for the encounter.

Slocum considered chasing after them and finishing the fight they had started, but it was getting dark and he saw no purpose in getting himself ambushed. Letting them return to their camp was dangerous, since they would report what had happened to Claymore and possibly Sheriff Pennant, but Slocum had no other choice.

He had driven them off, and for that he was glad, but Slocum realized he stood at the edge of a long and bloody feud.

12

Slocum reloaded his rifle, then went into the barn and took his balky horse from the stall. The Appaloosa knew he wanted to ride some more. Sticking around Finch's ranch wasn't too smart, since the three outlaws who had gotten away had at least two more in their gang. If Slocum counted Claymore, and he saw no reason not to, that made another trio of owlhoots coming for him. Better to hightail it to Woodchip than to let them find him here.

He rode slowly to give his horse the most rest he could, but Slocum found himself jumping at shadows and alert to every sound, no matter how small, if it didn't seem to belong. All that he ran across out of the ordinary was a large moose hunting for a nice lake bottom to nip at weeds.

It was close to eight o'clock when Slocum got to Woodchip. He rode past the Naughty Lady Saloon, and saw there was only a handful of men drinking inside. The promised whores had yet to put in an appearance and, from the way the men nursed their drinks, the prices were still sky-high.

The Fancy Lady was more crowded but lacked its usual gaiety. The men bellied up to the bar drank faster than those at the other saloon, but there was none of the usual joshing.

"John, you made it," Maude said, rushing up to him and throwing her arms around him. She hugged him close. He felt the hot wetness from her tears as she buried her face in his shirt.

"What's happened?" he asked, fearing the worst.

"Why, Finch said you were fighting off an entire army of road agents and didn't know if you'd ever get away alive. I tried to get a few boys together to go help but . . ."

"That's all right," Slocum said. "Finch was so drunk, he was seeing double. He probably thought there was twice as many outlaws as there actually were."

"You're sure?" Maude stepped back and examined him critically. "Well, you can use a bath, but otherwise your worthless hide seems intact."

"Thanks," Slocum said dryly. "Where is Finch? I worried he might fall off on his way here."

"He's sleeping it off in the back room. Sid said Finch was quite a handful this time. It was like dragging a bag of jelly. Never seen a drunk so bonelessly relaxed."

"He wasn't feeling any pain when he left the ranch," Slocum agreed. "Let's talk over there in the corner where it's private."

"We can go upstairs. To my room," Maude said. A sparkle came to her eyes. "In my bed."

"I need to talk right now," Slocum said. He had considered going to her room already and knew there wouldn't be much palavering once the door closed.

"Suit yourself, Mr. Slocum," Maude said with mock formality. "Sid! A bottle. Or whatever you got left."

They sat in the far corner of the room, saying nothing until Sid brought the quarter bottle of whiskey.

"We're running low, that I do admit," Maude said tiredly. "If we had a good night, there wouldn't be a drop of liquor left in the barrels."

"Did you order another shipment from Coeur d'Alene?"

"I sent a telegram but haven't gotten back an answer yet. I'm thinking I might mend fences with Ethan and see if he can't sneak me a keg or two. He might run the sheriff's saloon, but he was always sweet on me. I can cajole him into anything, if I put my mind to it."

"Won't do any good," Slocum declared.

"Why not? Don't you think my feminine wiles are up to the chore?" Maude batted her long, dark eyelashes in Slocum's direction.

"No," he said flatly.

"Well, I declare. You don't—" Maude stopped when she saw his expression. "What's happened to Ethan?"

Slocum explained what had happened along the banks of Whiskey Lake and how he had gunned down Ethan before running for cover himself.

"He wouldn't even talk? That's not like Ethan," Maude said. "Sometimes, I couldn't shut him up."

"He was protecting some secret at the lake," Slocum said, "and was afraid somebody would blame him for letting the cat out of the bag. I think Randall Claymore might be the boss, but he and Pennant definitely lock horns every time they meet. That tells me there might be a chance to split their forces."

"Claymore's men with him against Pennant's?" Maude sniffed contemptuously. "I'd bet on Claymore every single last time. Pennant is a fool."

"A fool with a badge and a considerable amount of authority in these parts," Slocum reminded her. "I have to avoid him or he'll arrest me for certain. The men with Ethan probably identified me, and they would tell both Claymore and Pennant about their fight. That'd be the only way they could explain away their injuries."

"You want to see if the doctor's fixed them up? Doc Goldberg might have overheard where their camp is."

"I didn't hit any of them bad enough for them to fetch a doctor." Slocum thought he had done more than wing one of them. A gut shot always turned fatal unless it was tended fast, but he didn't want Maude any more involved than she already was. Asking after the wounded owlhoots would only draw unwanted attention—from the sheriff, from Claymore, from the rest of the faceless gang of outlaws.

"That still ought to make it easier getting my whiskey shipped in from Coeur d'Alene," Maude said. "If you took out damned near half the road agents, they're not as likely to tangle with a wagon or two if there are armed guards along for the ride."

"How do you know your message is getting through?" Slocum asked. "Are you sending a telegram or writing a letter?"

"Telegram," Maude said. She scowled. "You're not saying that Little Billy is in cahoots with the sheriff? He seems like the nicest boy."

Slocum didn't know if the telegrapher worked for the sheriff or was only in fear of him. Either way produced the same results. And Pennant wasn't dumb enough to let any telegram be sent that might harm him or his interests. Slocum reckoned a telegram to the federal marshal in Boise would never be sent, just as one to Coeur d'Alene asking for more whiskey might be lost.

"I need to ride to Coeur d'Alene. Why don't I take your order to your supplier and hand deliver it?"

"My, what a fine courier I have," Maude said, grinning. "But it's such a dilemma. Do I send him with my order so I can stay in business, or do I keep him here and give him the business?" She rubbed against Slocum like a cat and almost purred.

"Let me get the order to your supplier and then we can really celebrate," Slocum suggested.

"You promise, John? You can be such a spoilsport."

"I promise," he said, giving her a quick kiss.

"Get me ten barrels, it doesn't matter what kind," Maude said. "You know how to dicker. Don't pay too much, because my credit's not too good right now after that last shipment was hijacked and destroyed."

"I'll do right by you," Slocum said. It took him another ten minutes to get free, but he had to admit Maude knew how to give a good send-off.

Coeur d'Alene proved far more prosperous than Slocum would have thought. The mining boom throughout the northern part of Idaho had brought great wealth to the town, and along with the gold and silver came merchants willing to sell supplies—and confidence men wanting to steal whatever they could.

Slocum rode straight to the freighter who handled Maude's shipments and went into the small office. He waited impatiently while four other customers were tended before he could talk to the agent.

"You want more whiskey?" The man shook his head. "I dunno. That's turnin' into a mighty dangerous route. It's hard to get drivers who want to be held up."

"Put guards on the shipment," Slocum suggested.

"That costs more." The sly look in the man's eye told how he was going to keep adding to the price until he made an indecent profit.

"How much more?" asked Slocum.

"Fifty dollars. Have to hire at least two shotgun messengers away from Wells Fargo for the trip. Can't get men who don't know the risks or who'd panic when they got shot at."

"Makes sense," Slocum said. Then a thought came to him. "Other than the whiskey shipments, how many other wagons to Woodchip get held up?"

Slocum read the answer on the man's face, though the agent tried to cover up fast.

"Why, the usual number. This is dangerous country. Road agents lurking behind every tree."

"None," Slocum stated flatly. "The only shipments that don't get through are the ones to the Fancy Lady Saloon. From what I can tell, the general store and the rest of the businesses in Woodchip aren't hurting for goods."

"Could be a run of bad luck. No telling what road agents think. Might be they have a powerful thirst."

"Might be they only want to destroy the whiskey." Slocum remembered all too well how the highwaymen had broken open the barrels rather than try to steal them. They wanted the contents spilled onto the ground where no one could drink it rather than to have it for themselves.

"Temperance Union?" wondered the shipping agent. "There's a strong movement of 'em over in Montana but not here in Idaho. Might be a band of renegade Mormons willin' to use violence. They don't cotton to any stimulants. Won't even drink coffee. Heard tell there's a whole passel of Mormons fixin' to come up from Utah, thinkin' Woodchip is their new promised land." The freighter chuckled at that. "Rumor goes that new logging will send the timbers down to Salt Lake City for the real building boom going on there."

"Ten barrels as soon as you can hire a couple guards and a driver who won't throw up his hands at the first sign of a man wearing a mask," Slocum said.

"That's gonna be money up-front," warned the agent. "Four hundred dollars."

"Half now, half on delivery," Slocum said, pulling out his bankroll. He had been hoarding his money but thought this was a good way to spend some of it. He peeled off two hundred dollars in greenbacks and dropped the bills on the desk in front of the agent. The effect of seeing so much money in cash worked its magic.

"Done. I'll have the shipment on the road within forty-eight hours."

Slocum nodded, then asked, "Where's the land office? I need to check a deed or two for the land around Wood-chip and Whiskey Lake."

The agent gave him directions, eager to get rid of him so he could tend the others crowding into the office. Slocum made sure the man had written down the instructions for Maude's shipment, then went hunting for the land office.

If Slocum had seen one land and assay office, he had seen a hundred. This one might have been a twin to all the others. A single-story building made from rough-hewn wood planks, it whistled tunelessly as wind wormed its way between the poorly fitted boards. Inside was as cold as outside, but Slocum wasn't complaining. The odor of chemicals made his nose twitch.

The chemist looked up from his assay work.

"What can I do for you, mister?" the man asked.

"I need to check on the ownership of some land down around Whiskey Lake," Slocum said.

The chemist put down a flask of blue acid, shucked off his heavy rubber gloves to reveal hands scarred from having too many chemicals spilled on the skin and began rummaging under the counter.

"Business is so good, I got to work twelve-hour days. I'm the only chemist who can do assay work, so the county clerk saddled me with the records, too. Made sense to him, even if it doubled the work for me. Here it is!"

He dragged out a heavy bound volume and dropped it on the counter with a crash.

"I got to hurry to finish my assay. Looks like some-body's going to be mighty rich. Could assay out to four ounces of gold per ton."

Slocum opened the book and took a few minutes working his way through the columns of names and figures before he figured out how to find what he wanted. Leafing through the pages, he found the section devoted to recording land purchases around Woodchip. He only glanced at the names, going for the area at Whiskey Lake.

Most of the names meant nothing to him, but one did. Randall Claymore.

"You do much assay work on ore from the Whiskey Lake area?" Slocum asked.

"Whiskey Lake? That's down south, isn't it? Some good mines around Oro Fino. Used to be a couple in Woodchip, but they petered out quick. Never seen a speck of rock from Whiskey Lake, though. That's not the right kind of geology." The man finished his worked on the ore sample and put it aside. He tossed his gloves onto the worktable. "I should hire myself out as a geologist. That'd make me a damn sight more money and save a lot of poor fools time and effort."

"What do you mean?"

"I could tell them the land around Whiskey Lake, for instance, isn't worth their effort. You don't find color in rock there. The mines in Woodchip were low-grade and petered out quick. They weren't hardly worth the effort. Nope, if somebody wanted to find gold, north of here is the way to go."

Slocum's eyes rested on the entries in the ledger book. Claymore had bought a considerable amount of land along Whiskey Lake, as well as three islands in the middle of the lake. Mining for anything on an island was a fool's errand. If the ore wasn't smelted on the spot, it had to be moved to the shore and that took some mighty big barges along with uncommon effort.

Every extra step in mining cut into the profits. The assayer had been right. A strike of four ounces of gold in a ton of drossy rock was hitting it rich.

Slocum ran his finger down the pages hunting for anything else out of the ordinary but didn't find it.

"Thanks," he said to the clerk. The man had already

begun work on another ore sample and only grunted as Slocum left.

Slocum stepped out into the bright chill of an Idaho autumn. He didn't know exactly what Claymore was up to, but he had a better idea. Whether this made it more difficult to get Claymore to sign the papers, Slocum didn't know. But he would find out.

13

Slocum fought to keep his eyelids from drooping. He could ride and sleep at the same time, and felt comfortable enough doing it astride the Appaloosa stallion, but he worried about being ambushed. In the dark he didn't stand a much better chance awake than asleep, but it made him feel safer.

The road changed from a deep double rut to a broad dirt track showing he was nearing Woodchip. This perked him up and even lent extra energy to the horse. It picked up the pace and almost trotted into town, eager for a stall in the livery and some much-needed rest.

"What's that?" Slocum wondered aloud. Ahead in the street gathered a shouting, shoving crowd. They all tried to get into the Fancy Lady Saloon, setting Slocum's pulse to racing. This might be big trouble for Maude.

He rode around back of the saloon, jumped to the ground and slipped through the storeroom to the main room. Slocum rested his hand on the ebony butt of his six-shooter, then relaxed when he saw there wasn't a riot going on. It was another of Finch's "parties."

Sid worked behind the bar, drawing beer as fast as he could and serving drinks that were mostly foam. No one seemed to take note of that as they swilled the bitter brew.

"Slocum," called Sid. "You want to wash them glasses? I'm runnin' out!"

Slocum considered stepping into the crowd and letting the crush of people hide him from the barkeep, then set to work rinsing off the glasses in a bucket of water before sliding them back down the bar to where Sid drew the beer.

"You don't have to do that, John. Unless you're looking for a new position," said Maude as she walked into the room.

"I like the old ones," he told her, grinning.

"Did you bring a couple barrels of whiskey with you?" she asked.

"It's on its way, with a couple guards fresh from working at Wells Fargo."

"That must cost a lot more," Maude said, frowning. "I don't know if I can pay it, but I do need the liquor. I could sell every drop in a dozen barrels tonight, if I had them."

"You're doing all right," Slocum said, his voice momentarily drowned out as the crowd let out a roar of approval and began slapping one another on the back. "What's Finch up to?"

"You saw him? How could you miss him?" Maude had to laugh. "He's a better draw than a dozen naked dancing girls. Well, almost," she quickly amended. "Pennant hasn't been able to get the women into his gin mill yet because of opposition from the townsmen. He might have the whiskey but we've got the entertainment." Maude jerked her thumb in the direction of a poker table in the center of the saloon.

Finch sat as stiff as a ramrod, his cards pulled close to his fancy brocade vest. A pile of chips in front of him told of luck being his companion. From the way his hand shook and his occasional listing to one side or the other, almost falling to the floor, Slocum knew the Britisher already had a snootful.

"Is the crowd for or against him?" Slocum asked.

"Does it matter?" Maude took his arm and steered him toward the stairs leading to the second floor. She stopped halfway up so they could look out over the crowd.

"How'd this all start?" Slocum let his eyes roam over the crowd. He recognized a couple of the lumberjacks and their camp cook who had bought the steers from Finch's spread.

"Word spread like wildfire that there was going to be a no-limit game here tonight. Finch was responsible for spreading it. I think he started drinking sometime this afternoon to get as loaded as he is now—and it's not on my whiskey, since I don't have any left."

"It's on the road, rattling its way to you," Slocum promised her, hoping that it was. Although he had considered staying to ride along with the shipment, he had wanted to return to Woodchip as soon as he could to finish his business with Claymore. Still, he ought to have brought a barrel or two with him.

Maude could make enough on a crowd this size to move on to a more agreeable location far from Sheriff Pennant and his gang. Let them sell all the booze in Woodchip. Maude could make a go of a saloon in any town. And there wasn't any good reason she shouldn't move to a larger place such as Coeur d'Alene if she had the money in the bank.

"Too bad I don't get a cut off the betting," Maude said. "I shouldn't get too greedy, but if I let Finch run a faro game, he might be able to pay for all his liquor and still come out a few dollars ahead. And I'd have a sizable chunk of money for the trouble of putting up with him."

"Loggers aren't as inclined to buck the tiger as miners," Slocum said. "They drink more than they gamble, or so it seems to me."

"You sound distracted. What's wrong, John?"

"I don't know." Slocum surveyed the crowd again but saw nothing to make him as uneasy as he was. Then the crowd parted enough to give him a good look at two of the men in the poker game with Finch. His hand went to the six-gun at his side.

"John? What is it?"

"The two across from Finch. Do you know them?"

"I may have seen them in the Fancy Lady before, but I don't remember."

"See how one favors his left arm? And the other moves as if it pains him? Those are two of the outlaws I winged out at Finch's spread."

"What are they doing here, playing poker with him? They have to know who he is!" Maude started down the stairs, but Slocum grabbed her arm and held her back.

"Don't rock the boat. They are mean customers. If you accuse them, lead will fly. It's better getting Finch out of the game. They might be trying to fleece him out of his ranch."

"But he's winning!" Then Maude got a horrified look on her face. She had worked in saloons enough to know how cardsharps worked. "They're letting him win."

"That means they won't take kindly to anyone pulling him away from the table," Slocum said. "They're building up his confidence in winning enough for a big hand he'll think he can't lose. They'll bet everything, thinking he will bet the ranch."

"What should we do?" Maude looked around, searching for any way for Finch to get out of the game.

"What if two gents started a fight right behind Finch? That would disrupt the game for a spell. If this kept happening, it might be hours before those two at the table with Finch moved in again for the kill. They're not going to let him keep their money. They sure as hell aren't likely to give up on cheating him out of his ranch. Buy another round for the house—"

"John!" Maude was shocked.

"Let Finch buy the round, then. Have him dance on the table. Do anything you can to slow down the play."

"Where are you going?" she asked. "You're talking like *I* ought to do all this."

"If two of the gang are here, more might be outside or in the crowd," Slocum said. "That means their camp is wide open."

"Delay," Maude said, more to herself than to Slocum. "We can do that. But what are you hoping to find at the camp if you're right and that all the outlaws are here in town?"

"Claymore isn't. I want to have a little talk with him."

"You think he's the leader and not Pennant?"

"I'll get out to Whiskey Lake and find out, if I can."

"All right, John, but it looks as if you've got the easier job of it." She hastily kissed Slocum, then went to cause enough chaos among the crowd to stop the game for a spell.

Slocum hoped she was right.

The rising moon cast a silvery sheen over the land and helped Slocum make better time getting out to Whiskey Lake than he had anticipated. He tried to keep the plat from the land office in mind as he rode, hunting for the property Randall Claymore had claimed as his own. Slocum got farther along the road than he had before, passing the spot where he had shot it out with Ethan Moore, and going around yet another sharp bend in the lake.

To his left were two of the three islands Claymore had staked out in his claim. The land along the shore ought to be his property, too, if Slocum's memory wasn't playing tricks on him.

He sniffed the air but didn't catch a hint of the bitter

stench he had before. But there was something else in the air that alerted him to the presence of men. A whiff of wood smoke coming from a direction away from Whiskey Lake drew him like a magnet.

Slocum wasn't too surprised when he found a well-travelled path meandering away from the lake to a stand of trees less than a quarter mile off. As he studied the copse, he saw a twisting curl of wood smoke rising to a height that it was caught by the wind and carried toward him. The path led directly for the source of the smoke.

Slocum dismounted and let his grateful horse take a rest. The Appaloosa found a clump of grass and worked at it while he slid his six-shooter from its holster and moved like a ghost through the night toward a small cabin hidden from sight by the trees.

The smoke came from a short chimney, warning Slocum that someone might be inside. He walked on cat's feet to the solitary window and peered in. A couple of cots lined the far wall. A table with four chairs dominated the center of the room. Other than the fireplace there wasn't anything else in the room.

Except the stacks of papers at one end of the table.

Slocum licked his lips, made a quick tour around the cabin without finding anyone, then gingerly lifted the latching bar on the door and slipped inside. The dirt floor had been scuffed up so much he couldn't tell if—or when—the last visitor had been in the cabin.

Going to the table, he leafed through the papers. A smile came to his face. Most were legal documents and all were signed by Randall Claymore. He was getting closer to the man. All he had to do was find him and have him affix his name to one more set of legal papers and his job would be completed.

Slocum never knew what warned him. He had developed a sixth sense for danger while serving in the army during the war, and he had come to rely on his instincts.

He whirled around the table and heaved, lifting it as a shield as a slug aimed at his back embedded itself in the thick wood instead.

Papers flew all over the room, but Slocum was more interested in getting his Colt Navy out and into action. As he reached for his six-shooter, a second slug struck him and knocked him flat on the floor in front of the fireplace. The shock of being hit paralyzed him. Slocum couldn't even twitch as he stared straight up at the roof. Insane, illogical thoughts went through his head. The roof needed patching. The floor was uneven. Someone would have to put the papers he had scattered back into order.

"You," came the single word, spat out like a curse. "Don't you ever die?"

Slocum's eyes focused on the man who had shot him. He recognized him, or thought he did. Slocum found himself in a curiously detached state until he realized he was going to die unless he acted— fast.

The outlaw lifted his six-gun and aimed directly at Slocum's head.

Summoning strength he hardly knew remained in his body, Slocum jerked his head to one side as the man fired. The slug kicked up dirt from the floor but otherwise went past harmlessly.

Slocum's finger tightened and his Colt Navy fired. He had not consciously aimed it, but either luck or instinct worked in his favor. The outlaw stepped back a pace, looked surprised and then simply sat down. His six-shooter dropped from nerveless fingers and his lips moved but no sound came out.

Rolling from side to side, Slocum finally got to hands and knees and pushed himself to his feet. He staggered, looked down at his chest and almost fainted. His shirt was bloody from the still-flowing wound. Slocum glanced at the man he had shot and knew there wasn't any more danger from him. He shoved his six-gun into his holster and tried to stop the blood leaking from his chest.

Slocum grabbed for the first thing he saw. Using a handful of papers, he pressed them against his chest. The first few layers soaked through with blood, then dried and began to stanch the flow. Slocum sat on a chair and regained his strength. Using a piece of rawhide he found on a cot, he tied the wad of papers to his chest. It wasn't much of a bandage but it worked.

Enough.

Stumbling out of the cabin, Slocum got to his horse. The Appaloosa stared at him with big, brown eyes but did not whinny in greeting until Slocum sank down, back to a pine tree, to recover his strength. The moon was climbing higher into the sky, casting an almost daylight glow over the land. Slocum forced himself to breath slowly, evenly, and felt his energy start to return. He knew better than to be lulled into a false sense of his own abilities with this serious a wound.

He sat a while longer, thinking about what he would do. In spite of the blood loss, his mind was clear and his thoughts razor-edged. Getting back to town was out of the question, but he could reach Finch's spread if he rode carefully and didn't get lost.

"The logger's camp," he muttered. "I can go there for help." Then he realized there wasn't anyone left in the camp. He had seen most of them crowded around Finch and his poker game. There wouldn't be anyone at the Rolling J, either, but he felt as if it was a sanctuary. If Finch hadn't already lost it in the poker game.

Slocum clawed his way to his feet using the rough-barked pine as a crutch, got to the Appaloosa and heaved himself into the saddle. The horse settled down, resigning itself to having a rider again so soon. Slocum worked to get a drink of water from his canteen, then urged the horse to head upslope. From the crest he could angle to the southeast and find Finch's ranch.

All he had to do was find the ranch before he passed out.

Slocum clung to the saddle horn and fought to keep from passing out. Before, he had worried about sleeping. Now the stakes were even higher.

He hummed one song after another to himself to keep his mind concentrating on staying alert, then forced his attention back to his path over the crest. The horse knew the route by now, but Slocum didn't want the Appaloosa wandering off course.

The horse lurched as it started downhill, whipping Slocum around. He grabbed for his wound and clutched the bloodstained papers to keep a jolt of pain from blotting out his senses. Slocum felt his strength fading so he put his heels to the horse to get it moving faster. He risked falling off, but he risked more by not reaching Finch's ranch house as fast as possible.

A small smile crossed Slocum's lips when, twenty minutes later, he saw the Britisher's corral with its three horses. He let the Appaloosa have its head now. Struggling with shaking hands and a head that threatened to float away because it was so light, Slocum pulled the saddle from the Appaloosa and let the horse into the corral with the other three.

He was as weak as a kitten now and couldn't pick up his own gear. He left the saddle in the dust as he made his way to Finch's house. Slocum settled down on the bottom step for a few minutes, then gritted his teeth and went the rest of the way.

Inside, he tumbled to the floor, crawled to where Finch kept his larder and found a bottle of whiskey. Slocum cried out in pain as he peeled away the paper bandage, then poured the potent, high-proof alcohol over his wound. He upended the bottle and finished off the liquor, then settled down and passed out.

14

Birds sang. Slocum tried to roll over and turn his head in their direction but nothing moved. He tried harder and felt a stab of pain that died away slowly. He sucked in his breath, felt the strain build in his chest and then relaxed, trying to let the air go in and out of his lungs naturally. Somehow, this eased the pain and gave him the idea that he wasn't dead.

Not yet, anyway. That meant he had the chance to even the score with whomever had shot him.

Or had he? The world was fuzzy and indistinct as he forced open his eyelids. Memories were vague about what had happened. It slowly came to him that he had already evened the score. He remembered falling down or being shot and stumbling after he had searched Claymore's cabin, then returning fire. He had done more than wing the outlaw who had shot him. Then he had hightailed it.

Why? His thoughts were jumbled and sticky, refusing to flow properly as he needed them most to answer his own questions.

"The wicked flee when no man pursues," he muttered, as he remembered more of the gunfight in the cabin. Slocum had known he could not stay there and had made his way back to Finch's spread, this being the closest thing to a safe haven he could find.

"You can be ever so wicked, but you have to be strong enough to do it properly," he heard. The words came from a distance, echoed around his head and slowly faded. He realized there was a ringing in his ears that almost drowned out everything else. Or was it the drone of insects? Instinctively, he knew it was not any cloud of bugs or anything else annoying. Quite the contrary.

Slocum forced open his eyes and smiled weakly. "Good morning, Maude," he said.

"Don't give me that horseshit about thinking you were dead and seeing an angel come down from heaven," she said in disgust. The small woman stood with balled hands on her flaring hips. "If you were dead, you'd be in hell shoveling coal to keep it hot."

"And I'd still expect to see you," Slocum said.

"I knew it! You're faking. You're not hurt at all, not with that sense of humor."

"Who's joking?" Slocum asked. He began tensing and relaxing muscles to figure out what worked and what didn't. To his surprise the only place where he felt much pain was in his back, where he had been winged by the outlaws earlier.

"Don't try to sit up," Maude said, her tone changing to one of worry. "You've lost a lot of blood."

"I'm all right," Slocum said, meaning it. The movement to swinging around and getting the wall behind his back so he could sit cross-legged showed him he was resting on his bedroll on the floor of Finch's house.

"Don't get blood on the wall," Maude cautioned. "It's the devil to get out. Whitewashing over it doesn't work too well."

"I'm glad you're so worried about Finch's decor," Slocum said. He pushed open his shirt and saw a small bandage the size of a silver dollar on the right side of his chest. He looked up at her.

"You're the luckiest man alive," Maude said. "The bullet went clean through you—and I do mean clean. Tore up enough veins to make you look like you ought to have one foot in the grave, but as far as I can tell the bullet didn't even put a notch in a rib."

She sat in front of him, the sunlight coming through a window behind her. The light caught the disarray of her brunette hair and turned it into spun gold. Slocum might have seen lovelier sights in his day but right now he couldn't think of what they might have been.

"You did a good job plugging up your own wound with these." Maude picked up a bloody wad of papers, then tossed them into the corner of the room.

"Glad I'm good for something," Slocum said. He sat quietly for a few minutes and then took the chance of standing. If he had lost as much blood as Maude thought, he shouldn't have been able to stand or walk without falling over. He was a mite wobbly on his feet but reckoned he felt better than the owlhoot he had shot.

"I do declare, being a nursemaid is all I've become. I brought Finch home last night because he was, in his own words, 'drunker than a lord' and what do I find on his floor but a bloody carcass—yours."

"Where's Finch?"

"Sleeping it off. He never saw you." Maude sounded more concerned when she said, "John, this is getting too serious. I hate giving in to Pennant, but I can't bear to see you shot up like this anymore. And with the whiskey costing so damned much . . ."

"What do you mean?" he asked. "I ordered a big shipment from Coeur d'Alene when I was there."

"Only part of it got through. The road agents shot and killed both Wells Fargo guards and filled the barrels with enough holes so I didn't get more than ten gallons out of the entire shipment. The driver said he's refusing to bring more liquor to me."

"Only the liquor and the men shipping it get shot up," Slocum said grimly. "I asked the freighting agent, and he said just about everything else reaches Woodchip without any trouble. In fact, he's shipping more and more here because there's a big increase in population due to the increased logging."

"It's Pennant and his gang's doing," Maude said firmly. "We both know it but we can't prove it. He's the sheriff, after all, and it'd be our word against his. It would take a federal marshal to bring that egg-sucking dog to justice."

"Pennant might think he's top dog," Slocum said, "but Randall Claymore is the one leading the pack. I'm not sure how, either."

"Don't worry your head over it, John. You rest up."

"Why would I want to do a thing like that?" Slocum asked, settling back down on his bedroll. "There'd have to be a good reason."

"I'll give you a good reason," Maude said with mock sternness. She towered over him while he was on the floor. Slocum surprised her by slipping his hand under her skirts and slowly running them up toward the woman's thighs.

"Oh, John, no, don't. You're not strong enough."

"I'm plenty strong enough," Slocum said, meaning it. "Are you saying you can't keep up with me?" He knew Maude could never turn down such a blatant challenge. And she didn't as he rose to the occasion.

She stepped forward so her feet were on either side of his outstretched legs. The lovely brunette began hiking her skirts, slowly revealing the white expanse of skin all the way up. She held her skirts in such a way that Slocum couldn't—quite—see the nut-colored fur nestling between those alabaster thighs.

He reached up and found the spot already damp with her excitement. Slocum ran his finger into her hidden recess and began working it around. It was as if she was the one who had been wounded. Her legs weakened and she slowly dropped down onto her knees, still straddling his legs.

"It's a good thing I got you out of your pants so you can get into mine," Maude said, reaching down and gripping the fleshy stalk that had sprouted from Slocum's crotch. She began massaging it, teasing it to an even greater stiffness. Rocking forward, she positioned herself directly over the purpled head on the shaft.

"I'm ready," Slocum said, but he quickly found that he wasn't. Maude dropped fast, her hand guiding him directly to the spot where his fingers had been a few seconds earlier. The sudden entry took away his breath and made him a little giddy. He worried about such lack of vigor until he saw that Maude shared his condition.

She swallowed hard, closed her eyes and tipped her head back as she moaned softly.

"So big, John, you're so big."

"Then I should ream out the hole a bit," he said, reaching down and cupping her bare buttocks under her skirts. Lifting until her hips were in just the right position, he stopped and simply enjoyed the sensations racing throughout his loins. Her nether lips parted around the tip of his manhood in a fleshy, wet kiss that nothing could duplicate.

Then Slocum relaxed and let Maude sink back down. She took him fully up into her moist, clinging interior.

This time Slocum made no move to get her to lift up. He reached out and unfastened her blouse, letting her scrumptious breasts come tumbling forth. He grasped them, one in each hand, and squeezed gently. Then he began moving back and forth as if he were milking a cow. He started at the broad base, his fingertips dancing lightly to arouse her. Then he tightened the grip as he slowly moved to the cherry nubs capping each of those delightful mounds of flesh.

Only when both nips were engorged with blood to the point that they pulsed with every frenzied beat of Maude's heart did he capture them between thumbs and forefingers and bend forward. Taking in turn first one and then the other between his lips, he sucked and kissed and gently aroused. Then his tongue lashed forth and dragged roughly over the sensitive nipples.

He knew instantly how much this thrilled Maude. He felt her powerful inner muscles clutch fiercely at his buried length, as if she were the one trying to milk him.

"Oh, oh, John, oh, aieee!" Maude cried out in release as he continued the assault on her sensitive flesh.

Slocum cupped her breasts and pushed her upward. This let his steely length slip from her insides until cool air chilled his flesh.

"No, no, I won't let you do that," Maude said, panting harshly. She flushed all the way from her face down to the twin mounds of her breasts.

She shoved herself downward and took him fully, twisted from side to side to add a corkscrewing sensation to the coupling, then rose with deliberate slowness.

Slocum knew she was tormenting him and returned the treatment the best he could. He felt his control slipping away as Maude moved up and down faster, with more deliberation, with greater speed and clinging power. He played with her bouncing breasts, then moved around to stroke up and down her back before moving lower to cup her buttocks. As she squeezed down powerfully on his buried column, he gripped at her fleshy ass cheeks. When Maude backed off, so did Slocum.

They began coordinating their efforts until they became one giant, heaving, single-minded body intent on nothing but pleasure. Sweat ran down Maude's face and trickled between her ample breasts. Slocum licked it off. Then it was the woman's turn to lick and kiss at his face. He turned and nibbled at her earlobe. She returned the favor.

And all the time she was lifting and dropping, taking him deeper and deeper into her needy center. Slocum was never quite sure when he found it impossible to hold back. He twisted around so he lay flat on his back, Maude still straddling his waist. She threw back her head and let out an animal howl that had to awaken the dead with its raw intensity.

Then she clamped down so fiercely around him there was no more holding back. He erupted into her viselike lair.

Maude rode out the intense winds of desire blowing through her and Slocum felt himself turning limp in her still twitching carnal tunnel. Then she leaned forward and pushed her legs out alongside his so she could lay with him. Maude put her head on his shoulder.

"You're so different from the others, John. I'll be sorry to lose you."

"You thinking of shooting me?" he asked. "That's about the only way."

"Right now," she said sadly, "but later? No, you'll be gone like the wind. The truth is, the wind's probably easier to hang on to. But that doesn't matter because I have you right now."

Slocum thought he would be tuckered out from the lovemaking but found it invigorated him. He didn't want to get shot full of holes again, but the thought was mighty attractive that this kind of loving healed him fast.

"When do you think Finch will have slept off his drunk?" Slocum asked.

"Ready for another round, John? You are amazing," Maude said, reaching between his legs and fondling the limp fleshy worm she found there. "What? No come-back?"

"Not yet," he admitted. "I was worried Finch might be awake and find us like this."

"I don't mind him watching if he wants to pick up a few pointers," Maude said. "Sorry, John," she said when she saw him scowling. "I was joshing."

"I know. It wasn't that, Maude," he said. "I was thinking of other things. Claymore is going to be hard to pin down long enough for me to get him to sign the papers I have for him."

"Is that why you're hunting him? Why should he sign anything?"

"It gets him out of legal trouble and lets his family get on with their business. A relative died and left a tangled legal web behind."

"If he's mixed up with Pennant, he's crookeder than a dog's hind leg," Maude declared. "You wouldn't have gotten him to sign without paying him before all the shooting started. Now that it has, you don't stand a chance of getting Claymore to sign any paper you put in front of him, even if you do it at gunpoint."

"That's a consideration," Slocum said. "He tried to rob Finch, and he's up to something out at Whiskey Lake. I just haven't figured out what it might be, though I have a good idea."

"I don't want ideas, John. I want action."

"Soon," he promised her. He pressed his hand into hers and then moved it away to give him more time to recover.

"That's the way everything's going," Maude said in disgust. "Too soft, too expensive, not enough. Especially not enough."

"You weren't complaining a while ago," Slocum said.

"I meant the saloon," Maude said. "What do you think I meant?"

"I know what you meant," he said, "but what's happened at the Fancy Lady? Other than the whiskey shipment being shot up again?"

"It must be one of Pennant's lackeys who came around offering me all the whiskey I could use—for a hundred dollars a barrel! That's five times what it costs to ship from Coeur d'Alene, but I'm not getting any through the ring of outlaws."

"So the hundred dollars is looking more attractive," Slocum said slowly. "After you paid Pennant the three hundred dollars for his license to do business, you didn't have much left."

"I've made a lot selling weak beer," Maude said.

"More than Pennant has made in his Naughty Lady Dance Hall, since he never delivered the women he promised."

"Finch has been a real godsend," Maude told him. "When he got Sid to play the piano loud and fast, that brought in the loggers. Then he started playing poker with more abandon than skill. Everyone wants to sit in since he gets so roaring drunk, thinking they can clean him out. They don't realize how much liquor it takes for Finch to lose all his faculties."

"The poker game!" Slocum cried. "I forgot all about it. What happened? Did those two from Claymore's gang win the deed to the Rolling J?"

Maude chuckled as she nestled against his shoulder. "I did as you said. A fight put the entire saloon full of lumberjacks outside until it was settled. When the game started again, Finch was in fine fettle. The two were letting him win smaller pots as they got ready for the kill. I asked Finch to dance."

"The two from the gang objected, but everyone else in the Fancy Lady wanted to see it," Slocum guessed. Maude knew what it took to get a room full of men excited. "That was a good idea."

"Finch and I danced for a half hour, but I saw he'd be out his poke and ranch the very next hand. So I did more than get him drunk. I had Sid put a Mickey Finn in his drink."

"A man who's passed out isn't likely to do much gambling," Slocum said. "Or complain about being kept away because he thinks he is riding a winning streak."

"You should have seen the looks on those two owl-hoots' faces!" Maude laughed as she remembered, then sobered. "I thought they might throw down on Finch, in spite of him being dead to the world, and shoot him full of holes. So I bought a round for the house and they sort of vanished." Maude heaved a deep sigh. "That about used up all the beer I had, too. But it was worth it."

"It was dangerous for you to bring Finch back here," Slocum said. "They might have been waiting to waylay you. They could claim Finch owed them the ranch, and killed you both. The sheriff would have gone along with anything they said."

"Everybody in the Fancy Lady would have known different. The loggers have as strict a code of justice as miners—or the Mormon settlers," Maude said.

Slocum let his thoughts wander a bit and then came back to the crux of the problem.

"I don't know if you can answer this," Slocum started.

"If I can't, I'll make something up." Then Maude saw the look on his face. "This is important, isn't it? Will it get rid of Pennant and solve your problems?"

"It might," Slocum said.

"Ask away."

Maude stared openmouthed at him when Slocum asked, "What does Woodchip do with all the garbage from town?"

15

"I didn't think the blood loss had affected your head, John. Heaven knows it didn't affect other parts of your body," said Maude. "But this is crazy."

"Quiet," Slocum said, pressing closer to her. The cold autumn wind had turned wintery after the sun dropped below the horizon. They stood beside the Fancy Lady Saloon, staring at a pile of garbage dumped out behind the café a hundred yards away. The wind blew in their direction, giving them a malodorous wait.

"What's the purpose? Do you think Claymore or Pennant will steal garbage?"

"Yes."

"John, really," Maude said in disgust. "I have to wonder if you are right in the head."

"You can go inside the saloon to stay warm," Slocum said, "or you can go back to Finch's house. There's no reason for us both to freeze."

"There!" she said. "There's Lacking Luke come for the garbage. They call him that because, after getting kicked by a mule, he was never quite right in the head. You and him have that much in common."

"Where does he take the garbage?" Slocum asked,

watching the burly, slow-moving giant begin to shovel the fresh garbage into the back of a small wagon.

"For all I know, he eats it," Maude said, her patience at an end.

"Get on back to Finch's," Slocum urged. "I'll meet you there when I've found out what I need."

"I hope you don't smell like Lacking Luke when you get there," Maude said. She hesitated, then kissed him. She ducked into the Fancy Lady, shaking her head in wonder that Slocum was watching a simpleton load garbage into his wagon.

Slocum waited for Luke to finish, then retrieved his horse and followed the wagon as it made its way through town picking up more piles of garbage. In Coeur d'Alene there had been garbage everywhere, but Slocum had been slow to realize that Woodchip wasn't similarly overflowing with the rotting debris.

Lacking Luke was the reason, and Slocum wanted to find out more about him.

The hunched-over man kept his mule moving at a steady pace until he reached a juncture in the road. If he had kept driving Luke would have ended up in Coeur d'Alene. The other branch went out toward Whiskey Lake.

Luke stopped the mule, got down and went to feed the animal a carrot. Slocum waited impatiently for Luke to get back in the driver's box and start again. But the man seemed content to simply pet the mule and feed it more carrots.

Slocum started to ride up and ask if anything was wrong when he heard the sound of horses approaching from the direction of the lake. He moved into deeper shadow, glad that the moon wasn't set to rise for several hours. He watched undetected as two men—the two who had tried to win Finch's ranch deed in the poker game—came up and spoke for a few minutes with Luke.

The man patted the mule again, then started walking back toward Slocum. He tensed, thinking Luke had spotted him. Luke trudged past, looking neither left nor right as he returned to Woodchip. Slocum let out his breath when Luke vanished from sight. He turned in the saddle to see what the two men from Claymore's gang did now.

One handed the other the reins to his horse, then climbed into the wagon and got the mule moving along the road leading to Whiskey Lake. Slocum smiled. He had guessed right. Rather than follow the slow-moving wagon, he cut across the ridge and came down on the far side, the dark waters of the lake stretching out into the night. The men had to drive past his spot, unless they left the road.

Slocum didn't think they would.

As he sat waiting for them, he saw a pair of small lights dancing about on the island nearest the shore. The lights moved about for several minutes like fireflies on a string, then vanished. Slocum grinned even more broadly. He started to mount and ride along the shore hunting for a boat to get to the island when he heard a man cursing and a mule braying loudly.

"Damned lazy beast. Move. Keep pullin', damn you!"

"Which one of you's the lazy beast?" laughed the man riding alongside the garbage wagon. "The mule's still walkin'."

"Not fast enough. This filth stinks worse than ever tonight!"

"All the better to whup us up some fine squeezin's," the rider said.

"For two cents I'd beat the mule to death and let the buzzards eat it from the middle of the garbage heap."

"If you did that, you'd have to answer to somebody a danged sight smarter 'n you."

"Claymore can—"

"Not Claymore," the rider said, laughing even harder

now. "I meant Lacking Luke. That's his mule."

"I ain't dumber 'n that half-wit."

The two made their way slowly along the road, arguing as they went. Slocum paralleled the road, taking his time to work through stands of trees and the occasional thicket. He eventually caught up with them. The men had stopped and pulled the wagon up to the shoreline. Slocum made out a dark shape moving like some sinister sea monster across Whiskey Lake, coming ashore to feed.

Slocum led his horse to a copse, then returned to where he could watch as the sea monster took on a different shape as it drew closer to shore. Slocum made out two men working paddles on a barge to guide it, with two more in the back pushing long poles against the lake bottom to move it along quietly.

"It's about time you got here. Luke got us a real smelly load this time," called out the man who had been driving. "I can't wait to get it piled up around *your* feet."

"Shut up," the man in the front of the barge said, lightly jumping to ground. He grabbed a line and began pulling until he got to a post buried deep in the ground that Slocum had missed before. The man quickly threw a couple hitches around the post to keep the barge from drifting away. The other three sloshed through the water to drier ground.

They worked silently and loaded the garbage onto the barge. When they were done, the leader made shooing motions to the two with the wagon and said, "Get it back to the dimwit. And check the load before you bring it out. We're gettin' too much in it we can't use."

"Only garbage, I know, I know," said the man in the wagon. "If this didn't pay so well . . ."

"Payin' the likes of you a red cent rankles," the man on the barge said hotly. "Get your asses back to Woodchip. We got work to do."

The rider and the man in the wagon got the mule pulling again and retraced their path along the road. Slocum let them go. He was more interested in watching the barge. All four men grabbed long poles now and began moving across the lake. From the way they worked together, Slocum was reminded of rivermen on keelboats.

Whiskey Lake couldn't be too deep, Slocum decided, or even those long poles wouldn't reach. But the men worked steadily if slowly and the load of garbage headed for the nearest island.

The island Randall Claymore had bought and recorded in Coeur d'Alene.

Slocum sat on the post where the barge had been moored and waited patiently to see where on the island the men unloaded their cargo. He smiled when he saw they went around the island where they would be out of sight should anyone happen by.

Getting to his feet, Slocum explored the shoreline and found what he knew had to be hidden there. Under a stack of cattails he found a small rowboat. It was leaky and rocked precariously when he got in, but the oarlocks were well oiled and made almost no sound as he began rowing. Now and then Slocum looked over his shoulder to be certain no one on the island had spotted him. Even if they had, they wouldn't know an intruder was on the way. They would assume their boss was coming out to supervise their work.

Looking carefully for the two dancing lights—from lanterns, not fireflies—Slocum finally stroked hard and beached the rowboat. He pulled it farther out of the water and then went exploring.

He hadn't gone fifty feet when he smelled it again: garbage mixed with something burning. Undercutting it was a more pungent odor yet. His nose wrinkled and his eyes began watering as clouds poured across the island before catching on the wind and being dissipated.

Slocum heard voices ahead and slipped through the

sparse vegetation, finally duck-walking closer to where a man, stripped to the waist, stoked a fire under a huge copper kettle. Coils came out of it and curled around finally to drip into a whiskey barrel.

Slocum had found Randall Claymore's gold mine. Claymore wasn't digging in the earth for his wealth, he was distilling it, and Slocum had found the still. His nose twitched again at the potent smells generated by the mash in the kettle and the way the garbage turned into alcohol.

When the barrel was half filled, another man moved it away and began throwing in rusty nails, horseshoes and anything else he could find to give the nascent whiskey color and taste.

"More water!" bellowed the man stoking the fire. "Get your lazy asses down to the lake and bring another twenty gallons. This batch is reducing faster 'n I thought."

"Get it yourself. We just unloaded another ton of garbage."

"Git!" snapped the man at the fire. Slocum took him to be the one in charge because he didn't see Claymore anywhere. Then he realized that the rowboat was probably left on shore for Claymore to come out here. But how many were in the gang?

Slocum tried to identify the men struggling with making the strong liquor but wasn't sure he had seen them before. That meant Claymore might have split his men into two groups. These who made the whiskey and the rest back on shore who kept shipments from Coeur d'Alene from reaching Maude and who did other odd, illegal jobs. They might even be working for Sheriff Pennant, for all Slocum knew.

What he was certain of was facing a dozen or so men intent on keeping their monopoly on the whiskey supply.

Pennant had ordinances passed making it illegal, then sold expensive licenses. And Claymore supplied the rotgut. The way loggers drank, it had to be a profitable oc-

cupation. Slocum wasn't sure why they weren't more
open about it, though. With an easy, cheap nearby source
of whiskey, Pennant could drive independent saloon own-
ers like Maude out of business by underselling and do it
legally.

But then, Slocum had found too many men who never
did anything legally if they could do it illegally. It was
branded into their souls.

"If you don't hurry up with the water," bellowed the
head distiller, "we won't be done 'fore sunup."

"What's the rush?"

"It's the Sabbath."

Slocum blinked in surprise because this seemed to
mean something to the men. They fell silent and began
working harder to fetch the water, to move the new load
of garbage closer to the still, to put their devil's brew into
sealed casks for shipping back to the shore at some later
time.

When that thought hit Slocum, he knew he had to get
back. He wasn't risking too much using Claymore's rowboat, but he couldn't get tangled up with these men. There
were too many of them.

He silently retreated, heading back to the spot where
he had beached his boat. Slocum slowed and stopped,
looking around when he got to the place and found the
rowboat gone.

His first instinct was to walk out a few steps into the
lake to see if the boat had somehow slipped it mooring
and drifted away. He held that impulse in check because
there was no way the boat could have floated off on its
own. A breeze whipped chilly and brisk over the lake,
causing small whitecaps to poke up, but it wasn't enough
of a wind to pull the rowboat out.

Fading into the underbrush, Slocum circled the spot
and saw what he had suspected. Two men crouched in
ambush, extinguished lanterns at their feet. They were

guards and had spotted the boat. Slocum saw where they had dragged it some distance inland and waited to see who returned for it.

Slipping his six-shooter from its holster, Slocum quietly made his way through the brush. Once he stepped on a dried limb but the men were too busy whispering to each other to hear anything behind them. They expected him to come from along the shoreline. Moving more carefully, Slocum got behind the guard on his left and judged distances. He wasn't strong enough to engage in a prolonged fight with either of them—and any gunshot would bring the rest of the bootleggers running.

He lifted his pistol and buffaloed the man. Slocum felt the heavy metal barrel crunch into the man's temple as it broke bone. Slocum kept swinging, letting the momentum turn him so he faced the other guard, six-gun level and ready for action.

"Freeze," Slocum warned.

The man was so stunned that he did what Slocum ordered without uttering a peep. It took only a split second for Slocum to step forward and smash his pistol alongside the second man's head, laying him out beside his unconscious friend.

Slocum panted harshly and felt weak all over. He wiped his forehead and then returned his six-shooter to its holster. Digging his toes in, he pushed the rowboat back into the water and started rowing for shore as fast as he could. The excursion to the island had taken more out of him than he expected. By the time he reached dry land again he was as limp as a dishrag.

Slocum didn't bother trying to hide the rowboat. Claymore would know someone had been out to the island when the two guards reported. The chance that they would come to and mutually agree not to let anyone know they had let an interloper escape was a slim one. Slocum reckoned the rest of the gang would find them and get the true story out of them.

Walking briskly, Slocum retrieved his Appaloosa and got his bearings on the North Star. The moon had yet to rise, but Slocum didn't need it. He knew the trails over the ridge and down into Finch's ranch by heart now. Even so, it took him a mite longer than he anticipated. Slocum had to keep telling himself he was still weak from losing so much blood. The bullet might have made a clean hole, but he needed to eat a few good beefsteaks to build himself back up and regain his usual stamina.

Slocum heaved a sigh of relief when he finally saw the rickety fence around the upper pasture on Finch's property. His Appaloosa easily stepped over a section that had fallen since Slocum had ridden the fence. He would have to tell Finch about this to keep what few head of cattle still grazed here from escaping. The logging camp would buy those beeves before winter smothered the land under its wintery blanket of snow.

Slocum rode around the barn to the front of Finch's ranch house. He was anxious to tell Maude what he had discovered on the island. He drew rein when he saw a man sitting on the steps, head cradled in his hands.

"Is that you, Finch?" Slocum called. He reached for his six-shooter, then relaxed when the man looked up. It was Finch.

"It finally happened, Mr. Slocum, in the worst possible way. My curse has struck another. I have grown used to the bad luck that follows me, nipping at my heels like some rabid dog, but now—" He shook a sheet of paper as if he could knock free the bad luck it held.

"What's that?" Slocum asked, dismounting. He was downwind from Finch and smelled the liquor. The stench was worse than at the still out on the island in the middle of Whiskey Lake. He took the paper and held it up so the first rays of the moon illuminated the crudely printed words.

"They have her," moaned Finch, before Slocum could finish the note. "They kidnapped Maude. And if I don't give them my ranch, they'll kill her!"

16

"Tell me what happened," Slocum said, scanning the ransom note, then tucking it into his pocket. He sat beside Finch on the splintery stairs.

"I had a bit too much to drink. It happens often, I know, but Maude offered to see me home." Finch turned and looked at Slocum. "She was going to meet you here, wasn't she?"

"I got some information I needed from her, then told her to get back out here because I thought it was safer than staying in Woodchip. I was wrong," Slocum said bitterly. It wasn't his fault that Claymore or his gang had kidnapped Maude, but he should have told her to find somewhere else, somewhere safe to hole up that the gang didn't know about.

"She drove me out here as I lay passed out in the rear of the buckboard." Finch straightened. His back cracked and grated as he moved, showing that the ride had not been easy for him, even if he had been unconscious. "She woke me up and helped me into the house. Then—" Finch shuddered. For a moment Slocum thought the man was going to break out crying.

"I need to know as much as I can if we're going to find her."

"We?" Finch looked at Slocum with bloodshot eyes. "You would want me to help you?"

"I'd take help from the devil himself right now to make certain Maude is safe."

"Yes, yes, of course," Finch said, sniffing slightly. He wiped his nose in a very ungentlemanly fashion on his coat sleeve before continuing with his tale.

"Maude made sure I was curled up all nice and snug in my room. I heard a scuffle some time later. Perhaps an hour or so, certainly not much longer than that. It might have even been less. I got up to investigate and found that." Finch pointed to the pocket where Slocum had shoved the kidnap note.

"It's not signed," Slocum said. "They didn't want to put it into writing who they are, but we know."

"The sheriff?"

"Sheriff Pennant and Randall Claymore," Slocum said. "They're in cahoots to sell liquor." Slocum quickly related what he had found after following Luke's garbage-laden wagon to the edge of Whiskey Lake. He concluded, saying, "I don't understand one thing, though. Why are they keeping this so secret? It's a legitimate business. They could have had their entire operation aboveboard and legal, especially with the sheriff's backing."

"Hardly," scoffed Finch. He stared at Slocum for an instant. "I say, you really don't know, do you? The sheriff is Mormon. All the men I have seen in these parts working for him are devoutly so, also. Their church would excommunicate them—I don't think they behead their sinners the way my church does—and that would be the worst thing that could happen. Worse even than going to jail."

"There are a lot of Mormons around?"

"Many," said Finch. "And more each day as they come here to supply lumber for their building in Salt Lake City.

I refuse to see my land cut down to build pagan temples there," Finch said stiffly. "My beliefs are at a variance with theirs."

"In a lot of ways," Slocum observed.

"They are strongly opposed to stimulants. That's the teaching of their prophet, Joseph Smith. I have had some delightful conversations with their missionaries on this subject, although none have been successful luring me to their ways any more than I have been in getting them to imbibe."

"So Pennant and Claymore are both Mormon?"

"To the best of my knowledge, that is so," Finch said.

Slocum thought about it. He had paid little attention to the rest of Claymore's family back in Kansas but remembered one saying that when the papers were signed, they could move to Utah. He had thought nothing of it at the time.

"Imagine that. Men who kill and rob and lie, but who fear anyone finding out they make and sell whiskey. Do they drink their own liquor?" asked Slocum.

"I have never seen them do so. In that they appear most punctilious." Finch laughed. "This is most peculiar. I am the world's worst drunk and a fine, upstanding, law-abiding fellow and they break every law in the world but fear anyone in their church finding out they are bootleggers."

Slocum thought he understood now. Claymore and Pennant saw the great potential for fortune as huge numbers of loggers moved into the area, but they saw it in selling a commodity their church strongly disapproved of. Greed and piety made for strange bedfellows in Woodchip.

"Where was Maude the last time you saw her?" Slocum asked. He wanted to get on the kidnappers' trail, and it didn't matter if they got roaring drunk or not. They had

Maude and had shown themselves to be ruthless in the past.

"Inside. She might have stepped out onto the porch for a breath of air. I realize how overpowering my, uh, aroma can be when I am in my cups."

Slocum got to his feet and walked slowly along the porch, using the bright silver moonlight to show the small details of Maude's shoes in the dust—and the other sets of larger boots. From the direction, more than one man had jumped over the railing at the far end of the porch. Slocum examined the ground under the rail and found hoofprints.

"They were on their horses and at least two of them jumped from the saddle over the railing and caught Maude. They dragged her back. They must have had a spare horse for her or she would have unseated at least one of them as she struggled."

"Perhaps she was held at gunpoint," Finch suggested.

"Why drag her if she was going, even reluctantly? She might have been tied bellydown across a horse, but however she left, no one stepped on the ground. There're only hoofprints in the dirt."

"Mayhap the horses covered those tracks."

"No," Slocum said. This was a minor point, but he was certain of what he read on the ground. The kidnappers had arrived on horseback and had left the same way, never setting foot in the soft dirt. "Get a horse. We're going after them." Slocum went to his Appaloosa and mounted, feeling the strain in his wounds. He was up for the hunt and the tired Appaloosa dutifully went along with the new demands of riding into the night while Slocum occasionally jumped to the ground to search for tracks. The moon was directly overhead when Slocum stopped and looked around. He had followed the tracks for almost an hour and knew now where they headed.

"Claymore's cabin," he called to Finch. The Britisher

drifted off to sleep in the saddle, catching himself with a jerk and then letting his eyelids slowly droop again. Slocum was sorry now for bringing the man along, but it had seemed like a good idea back at the ranch. Finch felt guilty about what had happened to Maude since he had slept through it without raising a hand to defend her.

Slocum doubted Finch could have stopped the kidnappers and would have probably been murdered if he had tried. That would have made matters even dicier since his ranch couldn't be deeded over without action from a judge.

For all Slocum knew, Sheriff Pennant might have a judge or two in his hip pocket. If so, killing Finch would have been an easier way to gain possession of the Rolling J. As he considered this, he wondered if there was anything more devious than the gang simply getting rid of a nuisance behind Maude's kidnapping. Finch acted as flypaper for the loggers, who all had taken quite a fancy to him. Get rid of Finch and a potential source of trouble might be eliminated in the timber camps.

Or it might be nothing more than wanting the forested ranch to sell trees to the lumbering company. Greed knew no bounds.

"Whass that?" asked Finch, snapping alert again. "Oh, yes, Claymore. You've found him?"

"The tracks are going in a beeline for his cabin. If I had known Maude had been taken, I'd have seen to it while I was over on Whiskey Lake." In a way Slocum was glad to have the time to settle himself, regain his strength and to do what planning that he could to save Maude. Barreling in would only get her killed—and maybe Finch and himself, to boot.

"I am ready, sir," Finch said, pulling out a rifle with fancy metalwork along the stock and barrel.

"Can you use that?" asked Slocum.

"I am a better shot than I am a rider."

Slocum stared at Finch for a moment, then nodded. It might be true. Finch continually surprised him with unexpected areas of expertise.

"I ride to the hounds, but I also am a fair pheasant hunter."

"That's not a shotgun," Slocum said.

"Anyone can hunt birds with a shotgun," Finch said in his haughty tone. "I prefer a solid shot rifle."

Slocum picked up the pace, riding over the piney ridge and down the other side, making his way along game trails and trying to remember the lay of the land. In the bright silvery moonlight, the forests took on an appearance that confused him just enough so that he emerged a quarter mile too far from the cabin.

He sniffed hard, caught the scent of burning wood and let this guide him back to the cabin.

"There's no telling how many of the gang are inside," Slocum said, studying the cabin closely. There weren't any horses staked out behind the place. He wasn't sure what that meant. The shack might be deserted at the moment, the gang elsewhere. Or Claymore might stable the horses some distance away to keep from drawing unwanted attention to the solitary cabin.

"I can stand watch for you and permanently remove any of those malefactors trying to follow you inside. Or I can ride in, a knight in shining armor, to save the fair Lady Maude."

Slocum made a wry face. Finch was making this sound too easy. Whoever went in to fetch the lovely brunette saloonkeeper was not going to do it without spilling blood—and maybe getting shot himself.

"You stay out here with that fancy rifle of yours. Be damned sure what you're firing at, if you have to shoot."

"The first rule of marksmanship. Never point the weapon at anything you don't intend to kill. I shall make certain of my target, Mr. Slocum. I always do."

Slocum checked his Colt Navy to be sure it was fully loaded, shoved it back into the cross-draw holster, then rode slowly toward the cabin. He had considered sneaking up on foot, but if the fat fell into the fire, a quick retreat on horseback might save his and Maude's lives. When he got to the rear of the cabin, he dismounted and flipped the reins around an ax-handle, the head of which was buried into a chopping block.

Making his way around the cabin, he peeked in the single window, chancing only a brief glimpse of the interior. That glance was enough for him. Slocum hurried to the front, lifted the latch and opened the heavy wood door slowly. A more thorough examination of the single room convinced him his eyes weren't playing tricks on him. Maude was tied and gagged in the middle of the room, secured to a chair.

Everyone else had hightailed it.

He went to her and ripped off the gag. Maude gasped for breath, then looked up at him with her brown eyes.

"What the hell's going on, John? They dragged me here and never said a word about what they wanted."

"They're ransoming you for Finch's ranch," Slocum said. As the words came out, he realized that wasn't the reason Maude had been kidnapped. She was bait for a trap. "Come on. We've got to get out of here."

"Where'd they all go?" she asked. "When they brought me here, there must have been a half dozen of them."

Before Slocum could answer, a sharp rifle report followed by a scream of pain told him the trap had been sprung—and he and Maude were still in its steely jaws.

"That's Finch. He said he was a good shot. Let's hope so." Slocum ran to the door and chanced a quick look out, only to draw a dozen slugs ripping through the wood all around him. He slammed the door and saw there wasn't any other way out of the cabin, save for the window.

Even as the idea of going out the window came to him,

bullets shattered the glass and sent shards flying throughout the small room.

"Get down!" he called to Maude. Slocum opened the door a crack and began firing at the dim shapes moving outside. He hit one with his fourth round, but Finch seemed to be having more luck. Slocum actually began to believe Finch's claim of being an expert marksman when he shot two outlaws in swift succession.

"Can you get the table and chair over by the hearth?" asked Slocum.

"The roof!" Maude saw immediately what he intended. She scooted the table over beneath the singing bullets coming through the door and the window, got a chair on it and hopped up. Maude dug her toes into the rock of the chimney as she clawed at the roof, tearing a hole.

"Get out. My horse is out back of the cabin. See if you can get to Finch. Just be certain he knows it's you."

"He's still drunk, isn't he?" asked Maude. "Never mind. I'll feel better not knowing until later. After we're all safe."

"Go on," Slocum urged. "Get out of here while you can." He reloaded and fired at the shapes trying to come in on him. "They'll probably try burning us out if they can't take us any other way."

Maude scrambled up and through the hole she had made in the roof. Slocum watched her trim legs kick, then vanish as she lay flat on the sloping roof. He heard her take three steps and then nothing. He hoped she had jumped from the roof and was already on the Appaloosa. The horse was gentle enough to not buck her off, no matter how spooked it might be from all the gunfire.

Slocum emptied his Colt into a man racing toward the cabin, a flaring torch held high. The man took a bullet, then another and another before stopping. He toppled backward like a tree being sawed down in the forest. But Slocum found himself reloading as another man scooped up the fallen torch and ran forward to finish the mission.

Slamming the door and barring it, Slocum started reloading his Colt Navy but got only one chamber charged when he realized he couldn't stay inside the cabin any longer. He slammed his six-shooter back into his holster as he dodged a bullet or two coming through the glassless window, got to the table and climbed onto the chair Maude had used to escape. He pulled himself up as the torch brushed along the dry wood wall and set the cabin on fire. The sudden blast of heat staggered Slocum and caused him to lose his balance.

Slipping off the roof, Slocum flailed in midair and then crashed to the ground. For a second he lay stunned as the conflagration consumed the entire cabin. He pushed to hands and knees and heard the sharp command, "Mr. Slocum, duck!"

He flopped back onto his belly as Finch fired directly over him. Slocum heard a man grunt in pain and then fall behind him. He scrambled along, digging his toes into the dirt for traction to get away from the burning cabin.

"This way," shouted Maude. "Hurry, John. There're still too many of them!"

Slocum tried to head for the woman's voice, but the crackling fire drowned out Maude's words. He rolled when tiny sparks tried to set fire to his shirt. The pain that stabbed into him from rolling around brought him fully to his senses. He came to a sitting position, spun around and thrust out his legs to brace himself. The intense fire burned at his face and forced him to look away.

Anyone caught near that fire was as dead as a doornail.

"Claymore," Slocum grated out. Louder, he shouted, "Claymore! Where are you?"

"Here, you son of a bitch. Why won't you die?" Randall Claymore limped out of the undergrowth a dozen paces away. He clutched a six-gun in his right hand. His left arm swung at a crazy angle and his clothing was scorched from venturing too near the fire. "I'm gonna kill you where you sit. You kept pokin' your snout where it didn't belong."

Slocum threw himself flat on the ground. His hand flashed for the six-shooter in its holster. He fired a fraction of a second before Claymore. Only when the hammer fell on the single round he had reloaded did Slocum realize how lucky he had been—and how accurate his shooting was.

"Claymore! No, don't die on me!" Slocum scrambled over to the man sprawled on the ground. By the light of the cabin blaze Slocum saw his single bullet had robbed Randall Claymore of his life. A tiny hole under his chin showed where the .36-caliber round had entered, and the huge bloody spot on the back of his skull marked its exit point. The slug had expanded as it ripped through Claymore's brain before blowing out a section of skull the size of a silver cartwheel.

"John, you got him. It was self-defense," Maude said.

"I needed him alive to sign some legal papers. He's not going to do much signing with the back of his head blown off."

Slocum saw Finch strutting up, the rifle resting on his shoulder like he was a soldier.

"We have run the brigands off. The ones I have not shot, that is." Finch looked at Claymore. "I see you settled accounts with Claymore, too. Thank you, Mr. Slocum. I am indebted to you for this service."

"John needed him alive to sign some documents," Maude said.

"His family needed them signed. Now I won't get paid," Slocum said. He wasn't one to wallow in pity. "I reckon I ought to take the body back. They might be able to get a judge to give them what they want since he's dead."

"You would have to explain how this miscreant died,"

Finch pointed out. "That could be quite sticky for you, Mr. Slocum. I, uh, have a certain suggestion to resolve your problem."

"What?" Slocum was in no mood to mince words.

"I have led a somewhat checkered career which, in part, forced my father to send me abroad to this fine country. One instance of my unfortunate past involved a touch of forgery. I am rather good at it, if I may say so and still maintain any semblance of modesty."

"You can forge Claymore's signature?" asked Maude, eyes wide with amazement at hearing of yet another hidden skill.

"His closest family members will be unable to tell the difference. Why, once I forged the Lord High Mayor of London's signature and found myself feted at Claridge's until the gentleman in question showed up to prick that particular balloon."

"John, let him. Claymore's family doesn't care about him or they would have sent a relative. All they want are the signed papers so they can go about their business."

"I say, Mr. Slocum, she is quite right. If they are anything like the unlamented Randall Claymore, they will desire a swift end to the matter and not care about legal niceties. I shall need a sample of his signature to study. A few hours' practice will be all I require before I produce a signature his own mother would be unable to dispute."

"That's fine, that's just fine," Slocum said glumly. "The only place where I could get a copy of Claymore's signature just burned to the ground."

Slocum stared at the remains of the cabin. The fierce fire had died down, most of the cabin consumed but embers still glowed red-hot. Dense smoke billowed, carrying skyward any hope of finding a paper bearing Randall Claymore's signature.

17

"We're not getting anywhere," Slocum said in disgust. He hobbled a bit as he danced through the still-hot embers left of the cabin. He used a long stick he had found to poke piles of ashes hunting for a sheet of paper that had not been too badly burned. It was a fool's errand and he knew it, but he refused to give up.

"How dare Claymore die like that?" cried Finch, striking a pose and staring heavenward. "Another few minutes and you would be rolling in the money, thanks to him. But no, he ups and dies, again cheating you of your due. For the beating he gave me, I should have been the one to confront him."

"Less talk, more searching," said Maude. She looked like some small animal come out from its burrow. She was black from head to toe, only her lips and eyes poking out from under the thick layer of soot. Maude rooted around on her hands and knees, hunting for anything Claymore might have put his signature to.

"No," Slocum said. "This is it. We've combed through the ashes and not found anything. As much as it rankles, I'll telegraph the family and let them know Claymore is dead, then ship the body back to them for burial."

"You won't have to go back to Wichita, will you, John? You can do it all from Coeur d'Alene?" Maude sounded pained and he knew why. She understood how he thought. Slocum wouldn't send the body back—especially one he had shot—without riding shotgun all the way on it. A thousand things might happen to waylay the body, and he didn't want that. While it was better to go ahead and bury the body right away, he could get a decent coffin and ship Claymore home.

He wasn't expecting any money from the family for shepherding the corpse, either. Slocum knew he would be lucky if he could lie his way around telling how Claymore had come to have half his skull blown off. Being sent to get a signature and ending up killing the man was far beyond what had been expected of him.

"Might be they have a coffin they can seal tight enough to make the trip back," Slocum said. "Getting toward winter helps, too."

"You could pack Claymore in ice," suggested Finch. "He always was a cold fish." Finch laughed at his little joke, then sobered. "There must be some way to get around this minor misfortune."

"No," Slocum said. "I—" He broke off his sentence, looked at Finch and then at the filthy Maude before letting out a whoop of joy that could have been heard all the way across Whiskey Lake by the men running the island still.

"John, what is it?" Maude pressed her dirty palm on his sleeve and left a handprint. "Tell us!"

"There's nothing here," Slocum said, "but there is back at Finch's place."

"The ransom note?" Finch asked. "But you have it in your pocket. There's nothing to show that Claymore penned that missive, and it was not written, but printed. Completely unlike a signature, I should say."

"Come on," Slocum said. "Let's get out of here and back where we can take a bath."

"I'm for that," Maude said. In a lower voice so only Slocum could hear, she added, "Together. Definitely together."

"Wait, old chap," called Finch. "What of Claymore's body? You said you wanted to get it back to the family."

"Let the coyotes eat it," Slocum said. "Or maybe his partners will come back and bury him and the others shot up in the fight. It doesn't matter anymore, not if I can find what I need."

Maude rode behind Slocum, and the Appaloosa did not mind the extra weight. It sensed they were heading for a barn with fodder and a stall where it could rest.

"What is it, John? Please tell me," Maude begged.

"I want to be sure when we get back," Slocum said. "I don't want to build up my hopes, but it's got to work."

They reached the Rolling J and tended the horses before going to the ranch house. Slocum opened the door and began poking around in the corners of the main room.

"Can we help you look for whatever it is you are hunting so avidly?" asked Finch. "I could do with a small squirt of a delicious amber fluid, but alas, I have none left."

"Here," Slocum said, finding a bloody wad and holding it up.

"That's the paper you used to stop the bleeding when you were wounded before," Maude said. "I don't understand."

Slocum began peeling apart the sheets. "I grabbed a handful of the papers from the table where Claymore had been working. There's got to be one with his signature." He held up a red-stained sheet. "Here it is."

"Do let me examine it." Finch took it gingerly and held it up. In the darkness he was unable to see well enough and went out on the porch to use the last rays of the moon. If he waited long enough the sun would rise and the Britisher could study it in bright daylight.

"I should heat some water for a decent bath," Maude said, "but I'm too tired."

"There's a stock tank behind the barn," suggested Slocum. "We can see if the water's clean enough for bathing."

"A wonderful idea, but I might get lost in such a big old tub. You'll be there to make sure I don't vanish under the water, won't you, John?"

"I say," called Finch from the porch. "This is a splendid specimen of Randall Claymore's full signature. It appears to be a land deed showing his ownership all along the Whiskey Lake shoreline."

"You can put his signature on the proper lines?" Slocum fished around in his gear and found the sheaf of legal papers. He turned them over to Finch, who handled them as if they were made from the flimsiest material in the world.

Finch carefully smoothed the sheets and examined the paper where the signatures had to be affixed.

"Pen and paper. I must practice, but it should not take me longer than an hour or two." Finch looked up and smiled crookedly. "That should give you and Maude plenty of time to bathe."

"Thanks," Slocum said. Then he went to tell Maude it was time to jump into the water. To his surprise, she was already naked and raced him to the watering tank.

The time passed too quickly for Slocum, but he finally climbed to the side of the stock tank and looked at a delightfully naked Maude paddling about in the shallow water.

"What's next, John?" she asked. Maude pulled herself from the water and sat beside him, her leg pressing warmly into his. The chilly wind kicking up drove Slocum to pick up his clothes and get dressed. Maude shivered a bit, then gave in to the weather, too.

"If Finch has done any kind of job on the forgery, I have to return the papers."

"I know that," she said. "What then?"

Slocum smiled. "Time will tell."

This didn't satisfy Maude but gave Slocum a chance to think about what he wanted to do. He would walk away from Claymore's relatives with another thousand dollars in his poke, giving him the freedom to go anywhere he wanted. Idaho was mighty cold in the winter, and Slocum knew people down in Texas he hadn't seen in years who would greet him with open arms. He glanced over at Maude and knew it could be even warmer here, in spite of the snows.

"Do examine my handiwork," Finch said, sitting on the porch with his feet hiked up to the sagging railing. He held up the sheaf of papers.

Slocum looked at the signatures, then at the legitimate one on the blood-soaked page. He shook his head and looked up at Finch.

"I can't tell the difference."

"No one can," Finch said confidently. "The only one who might dispute the signature is Claymore, and he is stone-cold dead."

"You are a man of many talents, James Barrington-Finch," Maude said with some admiration.

"I try not to dwell on my achievements," Finch said modestly. He looked at his fingernails, buffed them on his coat and then smiled broadly. Then his smile faded. "You are off right away, Mr. Slocum?"

"Reckon so."

"Will you do me a favor before you go?" Finch looked apprehensive.

"Name it."

"Allow me to see Maude to town before you leave. The horses need tending, and you are expert at such chores."

"How long before you get back?" Slocum asked.

"I . . . I will be back before you know it. I would appreciate this greatly."

"Go on," Slocum said.

"Excellent! I, uh, need to get some gear." Finch jumped to his feet and vanished into the house, giving Slocum and Maude a last few minutes together.

"I hope you'll come back, John," she said.

"Don't go getting into trouble before I do," Slocum replied. They kissed, then parted when Finch returned. His hesitancy before had evaporated, and he seemed buoyant now.

"It is so good to have plans and to know one's purpose in life," Finch said.

"You'll do good raising horses. You ride like an Indian," Slocum said.

"Yes, yes. Come, ma'am, let us be off. Time's a' wastin'!"

Tears welled in Maude's eyes as she waved good-bye. Finch took the reins and got the buckboard moving toward Woodchip. The way he snapped the reins made Slocum wonder what his hurry was. Slocum shrugged it off as he went to tend the horses. He made certain his Appaloosa had plenty of grain and was curried before moving to the three horses in the corral.

They would make a good start for a herd. The upper pastures were perfect for fifty head. It might take Finch a couple years to get that many, but these three were healthy, sturdy and the promise for a fortune that might one day dwarf whatever his father had back in England. The already insatiable need for horses in Idaho—in the West—could only grow. If the Mormons were moving into the area because of the increased logging, they would all need horses. Perhaps Finch could even raise a few donkeys and breed for mules.

Slocum mucked the stalls in the barn and did some

repair work after he had taken care of the horses in the corral. But as he worked thoughts began intruding that turned him uneasy.

Finch had been apprehensive, then turned almost cheerful when he had come to a decision. Slocum hammered a few more nails as he turned over what that might be.

He had thought Finch wanted to become a rancher with a vast herd of horses and had finally come to grips with what that meant. But was that what Finch really had meant?

"Come on," Slocum said, saddling his horse. "I have to head off a real tragedy."

He swung into the saddle and galloped toward Woodchip, hoping he would be in time.

18

Slocum slowed his headlong gallop when he got to the edge of town, dismounted and went the rest of the way to the Fancy Lady Saloon on foot, hand on his six-shooter and expecting the worst at any instant. There was an eerie feel to Woodchip that reminded him of ghost towns he had found where the entire population had simply decided on the spur of the moment, for whatever reason, to leave.

He rushed into the saloon and spotted Sid behind the bar. The barkeep looked up.

"Oh, it's you, Slocum. You startled me."

"Where's Maude?" Slocum asked. His mouth went dry when he added, "And Finch? What's happened to him?"

"You must have known he was gonna do it. Craziest thing I ever saw."

"Where is he?"

"He came in here, shoutin' out everything he knew about Pennant, callin' him out. I offered Finch a drink and you know what? He turned it down! First time I ever saw him pass up a free drink. I knew then it was serious."

"Where?" Slocum demanded, patience running out. He felt a coldness in his belly that wouldn't go away. Finch was trying to take the blame for killing Claymore and

176

damned near everything else that Slocum had done and was doing it by publicly accusing Pennant.

"Him and the sheriff and everyone else in town's down the street, out back of the other saloon."

"Maude, too?"

"Sure." Sid talked to empty air. Slocum was already racing from the saloon, the doors banging behind as he shoved them aside. He slipped the six-shooter out as he ran so he would be ready for the fight. He couldn't believe Finch was doing this, but there was no other explanation he could think of.

Slocum had seen his share of men in all situations. Some about to die were morose, others were emotionally deadened to the world; still others turned weepy and cried for mercy. But a few were strangely happy. Perhaps they had come to peace with themselves or maybe they were simply glad that their miserable lives were about to end. The excitement to greet death was what he had seen in Finch, but Slocum had not wanted to admit it to himself. He had let Finch ride off when he knew deep down what the man was going to do.

He swung around the corner of the Naughty Lady Dance Hall and saw a couple hundred people in two lines. Nobody stood behind either Sheriff Pennant or Finch as they faced each other, ten yards apart.

"Finch, don't do this!" Slocum called. He tried to interpose himself between the Britisher and the sheriff but Maude grabbed his gun hand and swung him around.

"John, no! Don't get involved. Not now."

"Finch'll get himself killed," Slocum said, but he saw that the two men were a ways from throwing down on each other. Finch had a holster strapped to his hip and a heavy Colt thrust in it. His hand rested lightly on the leather and seemed perfectly still. If he was feeling anxious, he didn't show it.

Sheriff Pennant was another matter. The lawman shuffled his feet as his fingers drummed a nervous tattoo on his holster. A tic under his left eye showed the strain he was under.

"Why'd he do this?" Slocum asked. He returned his six-gun to its holster but felt the need to shove Finch to one side and face Pennant himself.

"It was for you, John. He knew Pennant would track you down for killing Claymore since they were partners, so Finch confessed to the shooting. And he's confessed to a passel of other crimes to draw out the sheriff."

"He didn't have to. Let Pennant come after me. He wouldn't last ten seconds." Slocum felt a growing tide of frustration at being unable to do anything to stop the fight. "Pennant wouldn't have come for me. He would have tried to take over Claymore's still, keep all the money for himself and ignored me entirely."

"Finch is making that impossible," Maude said in a choked voice. "Listen."

"You call yourself a Mormon, don't you, Pennant? How do you explain all your bootlegging, all the illegal whiskey-making done by you and the unlamented Randall Claymore? That goes against your religion, doesn't it, Sheriff? Making whiskey and selling it?"

"Shut up," Pennant said. His hand shook a little harder now. "You can't prove any of this. You're just talkin' to make your own crimes look trivial. I never partook of a single drop of the liquor."

"No, Sheriff, that's not it. You might not have sampled your own alcoholic swill, but you're a hypocrite. You sell it, you make it, you own the Naughty Lady but make it seem someone else is running it."

"Finch," warned the sheriff.

"I'm guilty of killing Claymore. It was a fair fight. What are you going to do about it, you crooked, bootlegging, kidnapping hypocrite?"

"Don't listen to him, Pennant," called Slocum. "Finch

didn't kill Claymore. I did. It was self-defense."

"What'd I tell you, Sheriff?" said Finch, laughing. "He'll do anything to keep me out of trouble. That's the problem with having rich relatives. They can hire men like Slocum willing to take the blame for whatever I've done."

"He's lying!" Slocum was pulled back by Maude, who clung fiercely to his arm.

"You keep quiet," she said angrily. "Finch feels he's never done anything for anyone but himself all his life. Give him the chance to even the score. Let him do this for you, John. No matter what happens, he will be branded for killing Claymore and any of the others at the cabin. You're off scot-free. Let him make the sacrifice. Let him be a man for a change."

"But it's a lie!"

Slocum stiffened when he felt something cold and round poking into his back. The pistol muzzle touched the spot where he had been wounded, and sent a jolt of pain into him.

"I don't want to shoot you, John. Heaven knows you have enough bullet holes in that carcass of yours, but I'm doing this for Finch. He has to do this or he'll hate himself for the rest of his life."

"No man takes the blame for what I've done," Slocum said. "If he keeps at it, his life's going to be cut mighty short."

"Then think of Finch as finally becoming a man."

Slocum looked down and saw that Maude wasn't trying to decoy him. The derringer poking into his ribs was cocked and ready to fire. He wondered if she would shoot if he tried to push Finch out of the way, then decided not to take the risk. He might be wrong about Finch, as he had been before. The man was a superb horseman and his marksmanship with a rifle was about the best Slocum had seen this side of a trick shooter in a travelling medicine show. Finch might be quick on the draw, too.

Somehow, Slocum doubted it.

But he was going to stay quiet and let this play out. Everything Maude said was true. Finch would hate himself if Slocum intervened, and living like that would be worse than dying.

"You've got a lot to answer for, Sheriff," Finch went on. "You're the owner of the Naughty Lady, even if you've let other folks like Ethan Moore look like they're running it. Why couldn't you come up with a better name than that? Or did you figure you could drive the Fancy Lady Saloon out of business by charging outrageous prices for your bogus business license?"

"I'm a pious man," Pennant said. His voice cracked with strain. "I'm gonna run you in for killin' Claymore. You confessed to that and more. Might be you're the one makin' all that white lightning that's floodin' the entire region."

"No, Sheriff, I'm not the one making the moonshine: And I'm not the one destroying whiskey shipments from Coeur d'Alene to corner the market for whiskey. That's your doing, you and Claymore's gang. And Mr. Slocum's got a note in his pocket that looks suspiciously like one you would write."

"Note? What are you talkin' about?" Pennant's fingers ran up and down the length of his holster now, as if he would draw at any instant. Everywhere the sheriff's fingers touched leather, he left behind a smear of sweat.

To Slocum's way of thinking, it was closer to a snail's slime trail.

"Kidnapping, Sheriff. You were in on kidnapping Maude and using her as bait to try to kill Mr. Slocum and me. It didn't work. I was too fast for you."

Slocum heard the buzz of whispering in the crowd. Many of the townspeople were Mormons. From what Slocum overheard, they believed Finch was telling the truth about Pennant's dealing in whiskey and owning the dance hall. To them, that was worse than any of the other crimes Finch accused the sheriff of committing.

Finch was winning the war of words, but Pennant's nerve had reached the breaking point. Slocum knew all the telltale signs. The tic got worse until Pennant's face turned into a parody of itself, and then the sheriff widened his stance just a fraction of an inch.

Slocum started for his Colt Navy the instant Pennant went for his six-gun, only to find Maude hugging his arm close and preventing him from clearing leather.

The sheriff drew first and shot first, but his nervousness caused the slug to go wide of its target. Finch showed respectable speed—and dead—center accuracy with the six-shooter. He fired and the air filled with white smoke.

"You—" grated out the sheriff.

Slocum relaxed, thinking it was over. Finch blew the smoke away from the muzzle of his six-shooter and half turned as Pennant fired a second time. This shot caught Finch in the side and staggered him. He tried to speak, but the words jumbled in his throat as he sank to his knees.

"Finch!" cried Maude, rushing to him. Slocum whipped out his six-shooter and sighted on the sheriff, who lay in the dust on his side, not moving a muscle.

Slocum kept his six-shooter trained on Pennant until it was obvious the lawman was dead. Finch had drilled him squarely in the heart, but it had taken the sheriff a few seconds to die. Those few seconds were all he needed to trigger a second, deadlier round. Whether desperation or luck guided the bullet to Finch's side, Slocum couldn't say. And it did not matter.

He holstered his hogleg and went back to where Maude cradled Finch in her arms. Finch's breathing was harsh and rasping. From the bullet's point of entry under his left arm, Slocum saw that the sheriff had drilled Finch through both lungs, just under his heart. There wasn't anything anyone could do for him but keep him company until he died.

It wouldn't be long.

"You didn't have to do this, Finch," Slocum said.

"Yes, I did."

"Thanks. You're the best friend a man could have," Slocum said. Finch smiled slightly at this, as if it amused him or he had thought of something witty to say.

He stiffened slightly in Maude's arms. "My full name: James Matthew Barrington-Finch. Put it all on the gravestone."

"I will," Slocum said, but he spoke to a dead man. "I will."

Slocum looked up at the ring of citizens from Woodchip staring at him—and Finch.

"We heard it all," one man said. "The sheriff's not been straight with us, not if he's been making and selling whiskey he promised us that he was trying to stop."

"To hell with whiskey sellin'," growled another man dressed in logger's garb. "He's been double-dealin', killin' and kidnappin'. Didn't you hear what Finch said? The sheriff as much as confessed to everything the limey said."

"We're going to need another sheriff," said the grayhaired man who had assumed the role of spokesman for the townspeople. "Are you up for the job, Mr. Slocum?"

Slocum looked from where Pennant still lay in the dust to Maude holding an equally dead Finch. He shook his head.

"You don't have to go, John," Maude said. "There're any number of folks who travel back and forth to Salt Lake City. They can see the papers safely back to Wichita by courier from there."

Slocum smiled wryly. The local Mormons communi-

cated constantly now with the head of their church, telling
what had happened with the crooked sheriff and asking
what to do about it. Rumors had it they were getting another Mormon from Salt Lake City to take the sheriff's
job, someone less likely to make and sell the whiskey
their religion spoke against. Slocum wasn't much concerned with their spiritual well-being. He just wished he
could have stopped Finch from getting himself killed. The
one good thing that had come out of the man's death,
though, was taking the suspicion for Claymore's death
and that of the others in his—in Pennant's— gang off Slocum. He was free to return the forged papers to Randall
Claymore's family and collect his huge reward for the
chore.

Somehow, the money didn't seem as important anymore. Maude's suggestion about simply sending back the
documents and forgetting money was appealing. But Slocum couldn't do it.

"I have to," Slocum said. "I gave my word that I'd get
the papers signed and returned." He looked at Maude,
who had gone through Finch's funeral the week before
without crying. Now her brown eyes welled with tears.

They stood on a lonely stretch swept clean by a frigid
wind from the north, wooden grave markers scattered
around them on the hill. In front of them rose a chiseled
stone marker they had just erected, showing James Matthew Barrington-Finch's last resting place. It had taken
awhile to get a stonecutter from Coeur d'Alene to finish
the tombstone, but Slocum thought it was worth the wait.
No man could ask for a better epitaph.

Under Finch's full name was the line: COURAGEOUS
FRIEND.

"I sold the Fancy Lady," Maude said suddenly. "I figured a new Mormon sheriff wasn't going to let folks wet
their whistles in the city limits, no matter how much the
lumberjacks protested. First thing he'd do is clean up the

still out in the middle of Whiskey Lake and arrest any of Claymore's gang dumb enough to stick around. Talk around town is that the new sheriff will move the Fancy Lady way outside town, too. That wouldn't suit me, so I sold the saloon to Sid. Cheap."

"What are you going to do?" Slocum asked.

"Nobody wanted the Rolling J, it being so run-down and all, so I used the money from the saloon to pay the back taxes on Finch's spread." Maude smiled weakly. "I own a horse ranch now, complete with downed fences and not much in the way of pastureland. But it's mine, free and clear."

"Finch would have made a botch of it," Slocum said. "You'll succeed."

"It's going to be a lot of long, hard work," Maude said, looking up at him, her brown eyes glowing now. "I'll need a good foreman, someone who knows how to break horses, how to tend them." Maude licked her lips and tilted her head back slightly. "I need someone who can tend to my needs, too."

"The sooner I leave, the quicker I can get back," Slocum said, kissing her soundly. It would have to hold him—and Maude—until he returned.

Watch for

SLOCUM AND THE REBEL YELL

306th novel in the exciting SLOCUM series
from Jove

Coming in August!

**Explore the exciting Old West with one
of the men who made it wild!**

J. R. ROBERTS

THE GUNSMITH